ETERNAL DARKNESS

By Richard Terrain

Dedication

To my lovely wife Sabrina, my son Samuel and my close friends.

Richard Terrain
ETERNAL DARKNESS

TABLE OF CONTENTS

PRINCESS LUNA'S BIRTH

THE SHIP WITH BLACK SAILS

THE LAST NIGHT AT THE PALACE

FROM RICHES TO RAGS

LUNA MEETS INKYSHADE

FOUR BODIES AND TWO HEADS

DEATH BROODS IN THE FOREST

A BLOOD STAINED HARVEST

THE WEEDS THRIVE

THE BRAVE FARMER AND THE SAD CHILDREN

A LIFT WITH THE ENEMY

A GOVERNOR MAKES A DISCOVERY

THE CHILDREN DISAPPEAR IN THE MIST

THE WICKED AND THE GOOD

THE BEARDED MEN

Richard Terrain
ETERNAL DARKNESS

PRINCESS LUNA'S BIRTH

In the depths of space, far beyond the stars, which can be seen on a clear night, there is a star like our sun, and round this star the planet Tismos, with its four moons, is in orbit.

There are people on Tismos, created from the same stardust as we are, but they are so far away that they will never be able to reach us nor we them. However, if some of us happened to get there we might find ourselves in a forest with some of the birds and mammals we are used to. The people might make us believe we have travelled back in time to the days of farming communities. Tismos could be a paradise just as our earth could be, but reality unfortunately, is often different.

On Tismos there are many countries which are surrounded by high mountains and vast oceans. One of these is called Cestrelle and there the good King Jomar once reigned in a just manner over his subjects. He lived at a magnificent palace in the capital city, Lindby. His subjects were free and happy because the many centuries old power struggle between the Kings and the nobility was over. There was no longer any authority, which plagued the farmers with work and taxes. Under the threat of revolt and violence, the nobility had unwillingly agreed to give up all their privileges and abolish the system. Freedom was achieved a hundred years before King Jomar was born. The farmers and craftsmen chose the King by simply raising their hands at the court.

Lindby is a city in north west Cestrelle, beautifully situated by

the seashore, and many impressive buildings were erected there.
Two of them have given the town a reputation far and wide. The
royal palace is famous for its long rows of columns which support the
projecting roof, and many royal families have eaten their evening
meals on the terrace in the warm summer evenings. They could
enjoy the greenery of the Palace park even when it was raining. An
avenue of linden trees goes through the park to the palace and this
is the origin of the name Lindby.

The other famous building is a holy Temple in the centre of the
city, which is dedicated to Hindladrim, the Goddess of the moons.
Many pilgrims come to the Temple from far and near in order to
offer valuables in the moonlight. The inside of the temple is richly
decorated with divine statues and other works of art. The artificial
moons, with the four smiling faces of the moon Goddess hang from
the ceiling. Donations are made in the small courtyard, which is
enclosed by the walls of the Temple. According to tradition, this holy
building was erected by her godsons, who wanted to spread the
divine architecture to the human world. The temple soon became a
meeting place for travelling peddlers and the city grew around it. All
those who share the faith of the people of Cestrelle have heard of the
Temple of the four moons.

During this happy time for Cestrelle's people, King Jomar's wife
became pregnant and everybody in the kingdom waited in suspense
to know if the Gods would give them a Prince and Princess. They all
hoped for a girl as a Princess hadn't been born in living memory. In

the city the female fortune-tellers cackled like hens and spread the wildest rumours about the unborn child, but none of them was so sure of herself that she dared to wager her head as the old custom demanded.

King Jomar was not particularly pleased by the prospect of becoming a father. He thought he had enough worries already. It was no easy or pleasant task to reign over Cestrelle. His subjects were free; they could say whatever they wanted about his methods, and they did. Jomas was so irritated by the thought of being saddled with a screaming child, he wished it would die. Naturally he didn't reveal his feelings to Queen Shelana or to the courtiers, as it would have spoilt their pleasure.

One grey chilly day in autumn, his beloved wife lay screaming in her wide canopy bed. The great moment was approaching, but despite the pain she was as happy as a woman can be; her own child was on his way at last. Although Shelana was not a beautiful woman, he had fallen in love with her because she was as sensible and wise as a goddess. She was noticeable pregnant even at the royal wedding, which attracted some attention. Jomar also had a lovely young mistress, whom he met secretly, but her intellect was so feeble that he could never have married her.

The sky cleared during the evening; a cold night was expected and fires were lit in every home in the kingdom. King Jomar donned his brown marten fur coat and walked to and fro in the Palace park amid the colourful autumn leaves, muttering to himself. He was going *to miss the little freedom, he had and would have to work harder than ever. People would expect him to give a lot of time to his child's upbringing, but it was too early to complain yet. There was still a chance that the child would be stillborn.*

As the sun sank below the horizon he was surprised to see all four moons which meant a Holy night, as every child knew. The following day many of those who dwelt in the city would gather at the Temple and listen to the Priestess. Jomar was disturbed by the thought that his child might be born on a Holy night and he understood that it must mean something special. He no longer hoped that the child would be stillborn. If the Mistress of the heavens let the birth take place on such a night there must be a reason for it. Jomar felt increasingly sure his child would live and become somebody great, so he fell on his knees and prayed:

"Oh, Tismina, beloved Mistress of the heavens! You who gave birth to the Universe. Remove my evil longing and make me love my little one. Help me to withstand the heavy burden I must now carry. And may your blessing be upon us all. For ever and ever. Amen".

He had hardly said his prayer before the midwife rushed onto the terrace:

"Your Majesty, you have a sweet daughter, isn't that wonderful"?

The guardsmen heard the midwife. They lifted up their arms and hugged the Queen's maids, even though it was unacceptable to do this. One of the guardsmen took a burning torch and ran through the narrow streets spreading the good news. During the night there were festivities as never before and beer flowed rapidly out of the barrels. However, Jomar neither rejoiced nor drank; he went silently into Shelana's room looking very solemn. He finally understood that this was a great moment in his life, which he should have looked forward to during the summer.

When he saw his baby daughter, laying on her mother's arm, he was so overcome by intense love that tears ran down his cheeks. She was so beautiful that it was difficult to believe that Shelana was her mother. He just stood there crying, unable to take his eyes off her. The Queen tried to talk to him but he couldn't say a word. At last he lifted the child in his arms. She was warm and soft and full of life. He wrapped her in silk and linen and carried her to the window where the moonlight could fall on her sweet face. Now was the time to give her a name and with great difficulty he succeeded in saying: "My dear daughter. Your name shall be Luna. You are so beautiful in the moonlight. The Mistress of the heavens allowed you to be born on a Holy night of the four moons. Accept the love of Tismina and Hindladrim and let it remain in your heart as long as you live".

Jomar hurried to return the child to her mother as it felt cold in the Palace and she must be kept warm. Afterwards, he sat and kept watch all night as though he thought something harmful might happen. Shelana was exhausted and slept with the child on her arm. King Jomar soon realized that he was not the only one who was moved and happy; it was a great joy for the whole kingdom. He could hear the feasting in the city and drunken young men sang in the streets. Next morning the heralds would ride out to the villages in order to proclaim the good news to the farmers. The blue flag of Cestrelle, with its white wild strawberry flower, would be hoisted on every flagpole in the kingdom.

Jomar had only been sitting by his child for a short time when he suddenly heard beautiful harp music coming through the Palace halls. This scared him and made him think that the Spirits of the forests were coming to take her away. Luna cried but there was no fear in her voice. Perhaps she was trying to tell him that nothing harmful would follow the music. However, Jomar remained in a state of anxiety and he trembled as it came nearer. Supernatural beings were on their way and he hoped that they would be amiably disposed. There was nothing he could do.

He was startled when he saw the first Angel of the heavens standing in front of his child. The presence of such an outstanding visitor made him wonder who his daughter really was. Perhaps she was a divine being whose status was above everybody. The first Angel was clothed in a beautiful white embroidered dress and in her hands she held a burning wax candle. She smiled cautiously at him and said with a soft voice:

"You needn't be afraid. I have come here to give the Princess a gift from heaven". She turned towards the child, placed her hand on her forehead and said:

"I saw from paradise how enchantingly beautiful you looked in the moonlight, Luna. You will grow up to be the most beautiful Princess the world has ever known. Every young man will dream about you and my gift to you is beauty". The blond haired first Angel then disappeared and Jomar sighed with relief. His daughter had received the finest gift a new-born girl could get and there hadn't been any unpleasantness. The harp music was heard again in the palace and he understood that more visitors could be expected. Soon the second Angel of the heavens stood in front of his daughter. She was just as beautiful, but her hair was much darker.

"I shall make you into an intelligent and resolute woman able to reign over Cestrelle", she said.

The second Angel flew away on her white wings and Jomar was pleased that his daughter would one day get as far in life as he had, but he was also a little worried. It could be dangerous to reign over a country and the thought of his daughter being exposed to danger distressed him.

The harp music died away and Jomar was surprised when the third Angel stood by the bed. She patted the baby's cheek and giggled. She looked so kind that he understood that her message would be pleasant.

"My gift to you is love. You will love all your future subjects and do everything you can to make them happy. The people of Cestrelle will idolize you and one day you will be acknowledged as a Goddess who has descended into the world".

Suddenly, the Angel looked sad and tears ran out of her

beautiful blue eyes. Jomar couldn't understand why she was so affected.

"A time will come when you will be the only hope and solace for the people of Cestrelle", said the Angel on the verge of tears. Then she flew away as fast as she could. She didn't want to reveal how sad she was. After this the fourth Angel of the heavens appeared and went resolutely up to the bed. Luna looked at her out of curiosity but remained silent.

"I have come to give you courage", said the Angel with a melancholy voice.

"If tyranny and misery should fall upon your country, you shall not hesitate to lift the sword against those who are to blame". The forth Angel also began to cry and disappeared very quickly. King Jomar was terrified; he hadn't been so worried in all his life. He understood that the future would be filled with sorrow and distress. Those fortune-tellers who gossiped about adversity were right. When the fifth Angel came, he told her to return to paradise at once.

"I don't want to hear any more. It's enough now so fly away from here, please".

But the Angel had flown all the way from the heavens just to deliver her gift and she couldn't think of obeying the request.

"I shall give you a happy childhood little girl. Many interesting games and other pleasures are in store for you in the near future". But suddenly an uncanny feeling came over the Angel.

Something grieved her and made her extremely sad. She covered her beautiful face with her hands and cried in despair. The tears gushed through her fingers and Jomar saw to his horror that some of the tears were red. The Angel screamed and woke Shelana who looked up, drowsy with sleep. The unhappy Angel gradually calmed down and managed to say a few words:

"Well, at least the first years of your childhood will be happy".

After that she also disappeared. Shelana looked anxiously at her husband and offered him her hand, but Jomar only sat still and stared in front of himself. It felt as though a weight was pressing on his heart, which would crush him. Never before had anyone been as sad as he was just then.

"This is the punishment for my evil thoughts", he said bitterly. Shelana looked at him with surprise. She didn't understand what he meant. However, she felt the child was in danger and she held her arms around her. The sixth Angel soon arrived. She was already sad and she spoke with a sobbing voice:

"I shall give you a little brother to love above all when the time comes that you don't have a mother and father to love anymore".

Now began some unpleasantness. The sixth Angel looked very frightened and her face was deadly pale. She fled in panic from the palace as if before a hideous danger. Jomar suspected he knew who might be coming. There were only six Angels and after them there was only darkness, space and nameless terror.

A devil with huge black wings and sharp claws flew directly over the dark ocean to the Palace in Lindby.

Jomar gathered all his courage and shouted:

"Just come here, you devil. You needn't think I am afraid of you"!

Shelana was terrified; she looked at her husband and screamed.

She knew it was always wrong to invite any of the devils as it meant terrible things could happen.

The devil didn't come at once, but let Jomar and Shelana wait. Their anxiety and fear increased all the time. They feared for their daughter's life; they cried and prayed continuously. Suddenly an icecold wind blew through the bedroom and extinguished all the candles, It was pitch-dark except for the moonlight, which came from the window and had an unusual colour.

Shelana's beautiful mirror with its gilded frame fell in pieces. The baby began to cry and the wind howled. The curtains blew up and lightning flashed in the clear night sky. A gruesome anxiety affected everybody in the country. Those who were asleep had the most incredible nightmares and those who were awake felt that something was wrong.

The fearsome howls of hungry wolves, far away in the primeval forest, could even be heard in the city. A horrible thing then happened: the devil with his black wings and horrid skin stood before Luna. The little Princess screamed and Shelana tried in vain to comfort her. The iron grip of terror closed on them all. King Jomar wanted to drive the evil creature away, but didn't dare as it might kill them in a fit of anger. A hairy hand was placed on the child's

cheek and she was silent at once. She looked with astonishment at
the ugly face in front of her. Jomar happened to glance at the largest
moon he could see and to his horror he saw that it no longer shone
with its white light on the city. The moon was blood red and he was
petrified with fear. In fact, all four moons were red.
The devil had yellow eyes, which shone ominously. He looked at
the Princess and laughed crudely.
"Did you think you could avoid a visit from me, Luna"? He
grunted.
"I also have a gift. You little divine wretch! I don't like a Princess
to be born good and love everybody. Those white angels should never
have come to visit you".
The devil jeered so loudly that it echoed in the Palace halls and
never seemed to end. The howling of the wolves came nearer and it
sounded as if the fierce beasts wanted to come into the city itself.
The devil then gave his gift to Luna:
"I shall give you enemies who will hate you and try to kill you. I
cannot stop the people of Cestrelle from loving you but I know others
on Tismos who are not likely to do so. I shall make you mourning for
the deaths of those near and dear to you. Your whole life will be
filled with mourning and I shall send thousands and thousands of
misfortunes to your native land. Tears and screams will be heard
again in Cestrelle".
The devil looked pleased and flew away on his black wings and
disappeared over the sea. He left behind an unpleasant silence and

not a sound was heard anywhere in the Palace.

The wolves had gone and Jomar looked in despair at his newborn daughter. She lay quite still and for a moment he thought she was dead. But soon he saw she was alive and seemed quite happy. It was as if she had already forgotten all the dreadful things that had happened. Jomar calmed himself a little and tried to be happy, but when he thought about the evil curse he rushed into the Palace park and tore his beard.

"It can't be true. Who would want to hurt my little daughter? Nobody is more innocent than her", he shouted.

Queen Shelana cried the whole night, but the good Angels returned and comforted her. They fell on their knees by little Luna's bed, kissed her prayed for her and stayed with her. The moonlight was white again and nobody had any more nightmares. Everything was as fine as it could be.

Richard Terrain
ETERNAL DARKNESS

THE SHIP WITH BLACK SAILS

King Jomar and queen Shelana soon forgot all about the night their little daughter was born as they had so many other things to think about. Next day large crowds gathered in front of the Palace and demanded to see the baby. The King wrapped her in a warm fur and proudly held her on the balcony. He told them her name was Luna and they all cheered.

The most skilful joiner in the city was given the task of making her cradle and an artist from the country decorated it with gaily coloured flowers. They then delivered it at the Palace and both received a kiss from the Queen. Luna grew fast and was soon to big for the cradle, but Shelana gave birth to another child, a boy named Midar, who was two years younger than his sister and he took it over.

Princess Luna became the most beautiful girl in the kingdom with clear blue eyes and light curly hair. Her mother looked after her affectionately and gave her so much love that she couldn't be other than a kind adult. Nevertheless, it was the King who loved her most. Although he had to work hard to govern the country, he took every opportunity to play with her and take her for walks. He used to tell her that she was the sunbeam in his life. She gave him the strength to cope with all those troublesome and surly subjects who came to the Palace in order to complain.

He was grieved that Luna was a bit shy towards him, but it was *his own fault; he was gruff and dominant by nature.*

Prince Midar was envious of his sister, but he rarely showed it as he was very fond of her. She was his best playmate and always found interesting games for him. He was also a beautiful child with blond hair and brown eyes.

It was easy to see why the royal children were so healthy. Every morning they ate a health-giving gruel of the Gods. The court's chief cook was the only one who knew how to prepare it and he never revealed his secret. More than fifty children came up to the Palace every morning to eat gruel with the Prince and Princess. It wasn't possible for more to come as there wouldn't be enough gruel, so the children in the city took it in turns. The children in Lindby were often dirty, but before they came up to the Palace, their mothers used to make them have a bath and put on clean clothes.

The children were always noisy and excited when the gruel was served and sometimes the kitchen maids got their clothes splashed with the sticky stuff. Prince Midar was a real pest and when he began to splash it, all the other boys followed. But when the King threatened to make him stand in the corner, he calmed himself.

Afterwards they all played under the linden trees in the park. Princess Luna was very ingenious and devised many amusing games. It was soon time for the children to go to their schools but Luna and Midar stayed at the Palace and were taught by a governess; an old teacher who know a lot about life.

One beautiful spring day when Luna was seven, the governess came rushing in to the King's reception room. She was short of breath and the King looked at her with surprise. He understood that she had an important message as she dared to disturb him.

"Your Majesty, I think the Princess will drive me mad", she said. "I can't teach her anything. Every time I ask her a question she already knows the answer and when I try to teach her she teaches me instead. You should send her to the university now, even though she is only seven".

The King laughed and was pleased to hear that his daughter was so talented. Then he remembered that chilly autumn day, more than seven years ago, when Luna was born and received gifts from the Angels. The first six angels were kind to her, but the seventh, who came from Hell, was evil and worried him. However, he knew there was nobody in his Kingdom who hated his daughter and wanted to hurt her.

Luna and Midar were often free and the whole of the city was their playground. They ran in the streets and visited the large marketplace with its fish market. There was never any shortage of fresh fish, but the constant tough bargaining was hard on the poor fisher folk who were amazed that they were paid so little for such fine fish. There were many interesting things for the Royal children to see. They could go to the quay and look at the big merchant ships, which came from afar with valuable spices, but they got most fun by running down to the long sandy beach and taking a swim. They used to collect lucky starfish and look far out at the horizon where the sea meets the sky.

Midar wondered what kind of country lay on the other side of the ocean and Luna told him that she had red about a continent populated by cruel warriors who held serfs and beat their own children. No ship ever sailed there and the people of Cestrelle didn't want anything to do with them.

For every season Luna and Midar had their favourite occupation. In the spring they loved to run among the flowering lilacs and pear trees in the Palace Park. They went to the beach and enjoyed a swim in the sea during the hot summer days. The autumn was the time they went to the forest to pick berries. The winters were often so mild that there wasn't much snow, but when it was cold, they put on warm clothes and tobogganed down the slopes in the forest.

Luna had previously noticed, that her father always was surrounded by soldiers in blue uniforms and when she asked him about this, he told her that all rulers lived in danger and needed to be protected. It was like a sharp sword hanging over him on a weak thread, which could break at any time.

One late summer day, an old fisherman came up to the Palace and told the King that he had seen a strange ship far out at sea. King Jomar looked worried and asked him many questions. Luna sat nearby and was reading about the farmer's struggle for their freedom, but when she heard this she looked up from her history book and listened to the old fisherman.

"Your Majesty, we were all frightened. We saw that it was some kind of warship with black sails, which gave it a terrifying appearance. Furthermore, foreign ships don't usually sail in our home waters. They were flying black flags and every flag had a dark red square on it. The sailors looked strange and they all had dark red uniforms. They shouted angrily at us, but we couldn't hear what they said as they were too far away. It must have been a warship from that awful island. However, we brought all the fish home. Your Majesty can perhaps send somebody down to the fish market to buy some of our fine mackerel". Jomar was white in his face. He was more afraid than he would admit. Luna also became fearful when she looked at him. She understood that something was not as it should be. "Are you absolutely sure that there were dark red squares on their flags? Could it have been ordinary pirates you saw? They also have black flags".

"Your Majesty, I swear by all the Gods in the heavens that we made no mistake. There were black flags with dark red squares", said the fisherman.

"You can go now. I don't need to know more", said the King.

"Don't forget to send a servant to the fish market, Your Majesty. I am sure Luna would like fresh fish for her dinner".

He patted the Princess on her head and left.

Jomar called at once for his defence minister and Luna never forgot what he said to him when he came into the magnificent room:

"It would be best to mobilize Cestrelle's army immediately. We may have a war ahead of us"

THE LAST NIGHT AT THE PALACE

The darkness of the late evening had fallen over Cestrelle. The singing herds maids and the children who had picked berries in the forest had all returned home in good time. Those who were occasionally left under the dark fir trees and tall pines could be in danger. The elves and other small people of the forest entices beautiful children away after the sun had set. Many children who had been deceived by them lost their way in the forest and never returned.

Everywhere in the kingdom families sat in front of the fire in their cottages and farms. The old woman told the children fairy stories and mothers cooked soup on the hearth. Peace still prevailed. The young men thanked Tismina that they didn't need to be soldiers and go into battle. The wooden figures, which represented Derel, the God of war, were mostly forgotten in a dark corner of the Temple. Hardly anyone thought the future would be black. People took it for granted that life would continue with hard work during daytime and social life in the evenings. Freedom from slavery and need was the normal thing.

However, for those who lived near the coast, this cool summer evening was the last when they would enjoy peace. By the following evening they would no longer be free farmers and fishermen. Those farmers who lived further inland would get a few more days respite before they also met the same fate. The young girls loved peace and prayed for friendship between people, but a few years later these same girls would pray for war on their bare knees.

The royal family also sat in front of a fire at the Palace in Lindby. However, they were not as unconcerned as the farmer's in the rural areas. Anxiety had already begun to spread in the city. There were rumours that uninvited guests were approaching the coast. The bravest only laughed when they heard this. They no longer believed all the gossip about misfortunes and catastrophes. The old fortune-tellers had made up the most frightful stories but their predictions were always wrong, at least they had been so in the past.

Princess Luna slept by the fireside on her soft cushions, but before she fell asleep she heard her parents say alarming things:

"If the imperial army attacks us in full strength, how long can we offer resistance"? Asked Shelana.

"At best a couple of weeks, but if the worst comes to the worst, only a couple of days or hours. We have hardly any military power so we cannot manage a war", said the King.

Luna was angry when she heard this because Jomar had told her everything would be all right.

"You can rely on our brave soldiers to beat the imperialists. We are stronger"! He had said.

At the Palace there was grossly exaggerated confidence in victory before the coming trial of military strength.

"Our soldiers are as strong as bears and will do everything to protect us, boasted the ladies-in-waiting".

"If the rabble from Murtsch-Takesjdell come ashore they will lick the dust even at the harbour. Our soldiers will never let them reach the Palace".

Late that night Luna woke up and saw her father sitting in an armchair and looking straight ahead. His features were so solemn that she felt obliged to ask him whether he was angry with her.

"No my child, I am not angry with you", he said vaguely.

"I am angry with emperor Inkyshade, but I am not angry with anybody else in the whole world. Eat some of the fine shrimp soup and then go to bed and try to sleep. You will need your strength for tomorrow, as we have to make a very long journey".

Luna obeyed, but she couldn't fall asleep again. She lay awake for several hours under her flowery bed-cover. Suddenly she heard screams. She sat up drowsy with sleep, jumped out of bed and ran onto the terrace. From there she saw something which would change the whole of her life.

Down in the Palace Park there was war. Soldiers hit and stabbed each other to death on that same lawn where she had played with dolls, skipped with a rope and eaten biscuits. Men in blue uniforms fought with men in dark red. Maimed men lay under the linden trees writhing in agony and clouds of flies buzzed around their wounds. Luna herself was close to being pierced by an arrow.

"Go away from here Luna and hide in the Palace a soldier

shouted".

The emperor had so many soldiers and more kept arriving. A foreign flag already fluttered on a flagpole.

Luna ran crying through the halls of the Palace. She searched for her parents and her younger brother, but couldn't find them anywhere. She finally sat on a chair and cried inconsolably. She was alone in the Palace.

Suddenly, an enemy soldier came running through the hall. He looked around quickly and stopped by Luna who screamed with fear. He had bright golden buttons on a dark red uniform and looked nice, but she knew he was cruel and killed her father's men. Perhaps he would also kill her, but he didn't; he smiled.

"You are the Kings daughter, aren't you? We have put your father in a safe place so he won't be killed by mistake. He is waiting for you by the large statue. Follow me and I will take you to him".

Luna looked astonished at the handsome soldier who spoke with an awful dialect unlike any other. She had expected him to be cruel to her, but he was kind. He tried to hold her hand but she refused, as he was an enemy of her people. She gave him a surly look, but followed without saying anything.

"You are a sweet young girl so you shall have a chocolate biscuit".

"I don't want one and in any case not from you", said Luna.

The soldier roared with laughter.

"You are in a bad mood today"!

"Yes, I am and I intend to continue being in a bad mood until you have left my country".

Princess Luna and the soldier went through the large door and entered the park. The battle had ended some time ago. The small number of palace soldiers had not been able to put up much resistance and now the emperor's soldiers stood on guard everywhere. Luna wanted to shout at them, but she dared not so she had to be content with sticking her tongue out.

When she saw the injured and the dead being carried away, she began to cry again. One young soldier, who she knew, was bleeding from an injury to his face. He was in so much pain that he howled continually.

"You shouldn't be sad, Princess Luna. This is what happens in war and it's nothing to be upset about", said the soldier.

But Luna wouldn't be consoled. She couldn't accept that it should be this way.

When she arrived at the large statue she got another shock. The King was there, but he had been put in handcuffs like a thief. He spoke to her with an unusually mild voice:

"I am so happy to see you again, Luna. You have no idea how worried I have been".

"Why have they put you in handcuffs father"? Sobbed Luna.

"I am sorry it is this way", said Jomar.

"We should have tried to escape in the forest, but it was already too late when I knew the enemy had landed. We must now make the best of the situation and hope that they will listen to me. If the farmers in the interior of the country are unable to stop the attack we shall be forced to negotiate with the imperialists. Perhaps we must allow them to govern our country for a time".

"Where are mother and Midar"? Asked Luna anxiously.

"They are already in the carriage waiting for us. We are not allowed to live at the Palace any longer and the soldiers are going to take us somewhere else".

"Where"?

"I don't know, my girl".

Luna sat by her brother in the open carriage and they were driven away. They drove through the main street of the city, but it was deserted even though it was the middle of the day. The shopkeepers had closed their small shops and locked up. Nobody wanted to buy anything on a day like this. Everybody stayed indoors to avoid being killed. King Jomar's carriage was followed by several mounted soldiers to prevent any escapes and Luna realized that she was now a prisoner.

The journey continued through the city and they came out on a muddy highway. The birds sang as beautifully as ever; the leaves of the old oaks were as green and fine as on the previous day and the summer breeze was warm. But something was missing; the farmers weren't to be seen. They had been told that their farms would be burnt if they, or their workers, were found working outdoors before the soldiers had control over the whole country. Nobody milked the *cows, which were in pain, and nobody gathered in the harvest. Luna was sad over these quick changes and wondered what would happen next. She looked towards the city and saw black smoke rising.*

"They have set the houses on fire; they are burning innocent people alive", she called in despair.

"Be quiet my girl", begged Jomar.

"There is nothing we can do to help them and we can't talk freely any longer as the soldiers can hear us. It is best for us to remain silent".

The carriage rolled slowly forward. They passed a mansion where the flag of Cestrelle still flew on a white flagpole. The soldiers had obviously forgotten to lower it.

"Be happy to see our national flag", whispered Jomar.

"It may be a long time before you will see the white wild strawberry flower again".

FROM RICHES TO RAGS

The carriage with the royal family drove through an enchanting beech forest, followed all the time by mounted soldiers. The tramp of hooves echoed ominously and Luna couldn't reconcile herself with an escort just watching her, instead of protecting her; it was detestable. The whole family could be massacred whenever it suited the wishes of the emperor.

Luna and Midar knew very well that and old fort, with a moat and high towers, lay on the other side of the forest. The fort had always frightened them. They knew that swindlers and gangs of robbers were imprisoned there. The King also used to frighten them with this old fort if they got into mischief. He told them that disobedient children were sometimes made to sit behind bars there and were given a diet of bread and water. It wasn't until they were a little older they got to know that even criminals were given proper food and were well treated. King Jomar would never have believed that one day his own children were to be put in the fort and he was deeply distressed, as they were completely innocent. When Midar asked him why he should be put behind bars he couldn't give him an answer.

The trees thinned out as they approached the fort with its grey stone walls and Luna cried in anguish.

"I don't want to stay there", she sobbed.

Perhaps the soldiers will never release us. Suppose we must sit

in the fort until the rats begin to gnaw at our bodies!
The driver grinned and Luna became even more anxious, but
Jomar tried to calm her.
"You needn't be afraid, my puppet. I shall make sure they
release us soon. We may not need to stay more than a few days".
The carriage continued slowly over the moat and into the yard of
the fort. Luna saw that a large heavy grating came down behind
them and she understood it was almost impossible to escape. Some
of the soldiers pointed their crossbows at her. The mounted soldiers
followed them into the yard where they dismounted and tramped
threateningly towards them. The soldier who had been kind to her
was unfortunately not there. She noticed that these mounted
soldiers looked cruel and scornful. Never before had she felt so small
and afraid, but the worst was that hands, feet and heads lay on the
cobblestones, which were red with dried blood. Luna and Midar
screamed and looked away.
King Jomar couldn't understand how the enemy had succeeded
in taking the fort as it was built to withstand all kinds of attack and
long sieges. Traitors had either lifted up the grating and lowered the
drawbridge or the Cestrellen soldiers had simply run away. The
present soldiers saw that Jomar was bewildered and they laughed at
him.
"There is not much left of your cowardly hares, sneered one of
them".
"Shall we give the poor king a little present? said another".

"He may need some encouragement now that he has been dethroned".

One of the heads was thrown to Jomar. Then they ripped off his magnificent gold crown and threw it into the muddy water of the moat. Shelana and Luna fell into each other's arms in grief. From that moment Cestrelle ceased to exist. The beloved countryside was now just a region in the Murtsch-Takesjdell empire. Jomar and his family were told to follow their warders. Luna saw that a small cottage with thatched roof lay near the wall and she dearly hoped they would be allowed to live there. But they were forced to go through an iron door and climb seventy steps up some narrow stone stairs. They were to be confined in a room in one of the high towers. An iron door slammed behind them and a key was turned in the lock.

The whole family were put in a small room with stone walls and a stone floor. There was no furniture and the floor was covered in straw on which they had to sleep. An old stone jar, which was placed by the iron door, contained their fly infested drinking water and their toilet consisted of a rusty bucket by the wall.

It was dark in their ghastly room, but some light entered through a small window opening and Luna could just push her head through it. She saw how the emperor's soldiers were drilled by an officer in the yard. If Luna hadn't been so sad, she would probably have laughed at them as they looked more like marionettes than human beings.

Jomar held something, which glittered and Luna asked him what it was.

"It is a gift which I shall probably have to give you my girl", he said with sadness in his voice.

"If I and your mother have to die you will get this magic stone to protect you and Midar against all the evil in the world".

Luna was so tired that she couldn't cry anymore. They hadn't had any food today and they were hungry. The warders threw in some bits of very salty meat, which lay on the dirty stone floor. There were no plates and no cutlery.

"These soldiers think that prisoners should be treated like animals, complained Shelana. Luna longed for the good gruel they had eaten at the palace; perhaps she would never taste it again. Shouting and commotion could be heard later from the yard. Luna looked through the opening and saw many men with tattered clothes staggering joyfully out of the underground dungeon. They praised the soldiers and called them liberators. Then they saw semi-nude men and women coming in over the drawbridge followed by soldiers. These new prisoners had been put in iron and many of them were crying. Some of them had gory sores on their backs, caused by whiplashes, and the soldiers compelled them to go down into the dungeon.

Luna understood exactly what had happened. The imperial soldiers had taken so many prisoners that they were compelled to release some of the thieves. It was cunning of the emperor to liberate the thieves, as he would then get support from the criminals. The new prisoners were honest people.

It was evening again with half-starvation and stench. So far nobody had told the family why they had been imprisoned nor what was going to happen to them. In Luna's history book it said that people who are free and can chose their own King are stronger than those who are enslaved. But now she saw that the books were wrong and she wondered why she had been taught things which were not in accordance with reality.

"I earnestly wish the book had been right", she whispered.

LUNA MEETS INKYSHADE

A mounted enemy officer with a disfigured face galloped along the road through the beech forest. He was in such a hurry that he had left his guard of honour behind him and when he saw that he was alone he became terribly frightened. He was in a foreign country where he didn't feel safe and secure. He looked anxiously around to see if there were any enemies in the vicinity and although he didn't see any he knew they could be lying in wait in the thickets.

The enemy in blue uniform was determined to get him and wouldn't give up until he was dead and buried. Inkyshade didn't even trust his own soldiers. If it wasn't for their fear of the whip and the red-hot iron, they would have stabbed him to death in order to get more power for themselves. Inkyshade had no nose and there were just two ugly holes where it should have been. His nose had been bitten off by a shoal of predatory fish when his father, the late emperor Inkyshade, had let him bathe in a dangerous lake as a punishment for being coward. Most of the people in Murtsch-Takesjdell however had their noses intact!

The nose less emperor sighed with relief when he saw the grey walls of the fort in front of him. Inside those walls he could feel safe at last. It was his dream to spend the rest of his life in a fort and be waited on by serfs. He could govern his immense empire from a fort without being attacked by bloodthirsty peasants. When the war was over he intended to have the strongest fort in the world.

However, the emperor had other concerns. Above all he loved gold, but he didn't own much of it.

"I hope they can find gold here he thought".

"Otherwise there is no point in crushing this country". Inkyshade had to solve one more problem before he could think about gold. His soldiers had arrested the royal family and it was necessary to decide their fate. He, of course, wanted to behead them all, but first he must consult his admirals and generals. Hopefully, they were clever enough to decide if such an execution was advisable.

The soldiers greeted their emperor with deep bows and Inkyshade enjoyed seeing their humility.

"The day will come when everybody in the world will bow to me and pay homage to me", he cried.

When he saw the gory heads, which lay on the yard, a revolting smile crossed his lips.

"This is what will happen to all those who don't like me", he roared.

The soldiers invited him to enter a large stone room where the officers of the high command already sat and waited. They stood up when he entered.

"Congratulations, your Imperial Majesty", said the senior general with a false smile.

"You have already had great success in the war and shown that you are the greatest of all military commanders. We have arrested the whole royal family for you".

"That wasn't any news for me", sneered Inkyshade, who saw that the general was false.

It irritated him that people were so sly.

"I shall compel everybody to be honest and behave in a natural way", he thought.

A servant came in with a dram of schnapps. Inkyshade took his drink but didn't look at the servant as he was a vile person.

"Well, where is that dangerous King Jomar and his family", he shouted.

The senior general understood that there was no point in ingratiating himself so he answered with a harsh voice:

"I have imprisoned them in the tower here, your Imperial Majesty".

Inkyshade looked in terror at the general. He jumped up from his chair and hid behind a door where he stood and trembled for a long time before he dared to step out.

"Are they really here at the tower"? He said anxiously.

"Why didn't you tell me before? My life is in danger, but it doesn't seem to disturb you at all. The King could escape and kill me".

Here was the man who said that he was the bravest in the world and yet he behaved like frightened little rabbit. One of the officers couldn't help putting on a scornful smile and unfortunately Inkyshade saw him. It angered him so much that he lost his temper and punched the officer on his mouth and he fell down.

"You dare to sneer at your emperor? You think I am a coward. I shall slice you into four pieces", bellowed Inkyshade.

Then, unexpectedly, he calmed down.

"I need some sound advice from you officers. What do you think I should do with King Jomar and his family"?

"I suggest that you allow them to return to their palace, your imperial majesty. But first you must be certain that they will accept your authority and not incite the people to revolt", said the senior general.

This answer was unexpected and Inkyshade became furious again. He wanted to hear a wise man say that the royal family should be executed.

"You are nothing but a traitor", he shouted at the general.

"You know very well what will happen if I let the royal family live. Sooner or later they will overthrow me. People of royal lineage are highly dangerous. They should all be killed. Of course I don't mean myself! There is a difference between royal and imperial lineage".

"I must say what I think, your imperial majesty", said a redbearded admiral, who spoke for the first time.

"In my opinion it would be very distasteful of you to behead the royal children. Only a tyrant would do such a thing and you have often said that you don't want to be a tyrant. For safety's sake though, I think you should behead King Jomar and Queen Shelana".

Inkyshade looked at him scornfully.

"Well spoken! You really are a talented man dear Roxpashleix. If I let the Prince and Princess live, but execute their parents they will of course love me above all. They will be my most loyal servants and never think about revenge. You blackguard! You would like to see me dead".

Jomar, Shelana, Luna and Midar then received their sentences. Inkyshade intoned solemnly and malevolently:

"I, emperor Inkyshade, hereby decree that King Jomar and Queen Shelana shall be beheaded at dawn. Prince Midar and Princess Luna shall also be beheaded at that time".

"I hope Tismina will forgive me for this evil deed. The executions must be carried out".

A key was placed in Inkyshade's hand. He then left his staff officers and walked slowly up the narrow dark steps in the tower. He intended to tell the royal family himself about their fate and he was curious to see how they all looked. When Inkyshade was sufficiently worked up his fear disappeared and he forgot that people could be dangerous.

Luna was dozing with her head on her mother's knee when a key was suddenly put in the lock on the iron door. She looked up hopefully. Perhaps somebody had come to release them, but the next instant she screamed with terror. It was Inkyshade; she saw his disfigured face for the first time. The stately uniform with its orders and medals couldn't conceal the fact that it was worn by a human monster of the worst kind.

"Who are you and what brings you here"? Asked Jomar sharply.

"I am emperor Inkyshade and I am the ruler of the lands on both sides of the ocean".

He then slammed the iron door behind him and stood in the middle of the floor, but to his great surprise the Princess rose up and rushed at him.

"My father was chosen by the people", she shouted.

"You have no right to rule Cestrelle and you have no right to keep us locked up. You are a wicked and disgusting person"!

She hit him and beat on his uniform with her small fists.

Inkyshade fled in panic down the stairs without locking the door and his soldiers had to take the escaping family up the tower again.

"It will soon be the end for all of you", screamed Inkyshade from the yard.

"You shall die, King Jomar. Your consort and your son shall also die. Your disorderly daughter will suffer the same fate".

Luna heard the tyrant's scream, but strangely enough she wasn't afraid when she heard her own death sentence. She only felt that a melancholy fire had begun deep inside her.

"When we die, we die for Cestrelle, for freedom and for the whole of mankind", said Jomar trembling.

"Our blood will be a call to everybody to continue the fight until the world is liberated from this dark tyranny. One day the rulers of Murtsch-Takesjdell will see our victory".

"How can we die for Cestrelle when it no longer exists"? said

Shelana.

"You saw what happened to your gold crown. Freedom is dead for ever. This is the bitter end not only for us, but also for our compatriots and the whole world".

"It is not the end", insisted Jomar.

"Perhaps my death and your death don't mean so much, but from our beloved Luna's cruel fate something great will come".

An hour later two soldiers went up to the tower with a letter to Jomar which carried the imperial seal and was written by Inkyshade. It was a most evil and terrifying letter.

To King Jomar,

As Princess Luna has shown herself to be exceptionally illmannered and ill-bred, I have decided to punish her in the following way:

When you and your consort have been beheaded, the coffins containing your dead bodies will be carried up the tower together with a sack containing your heads. Princess Luna will be imprisoned all night together with your corpses before she is executed. Your little son will be allowed to choose between execution at the first opportunity or the latter.

Signed: emperor Inkyshade.

Luna gazed sadly at her beloved parents and fell into tears. She was so desperately unhappy that she thought she would die immediately and Shelana hugged her tightly for a long time. Jomar felt that he had never loved Luna so much as during these agonizing days.

"This is the work of the devil, he said quietly".

"The evil prophecy has come true at last".

Later in the evening a soldier threw in some salted herring which Luna picked up and dropped through the window opening in the hope that it would hit some of the hated soldiers in the yard below.

It began to rain. It was a real cloudburst and cold air came in which increased their agony, but there were others who suffered even more. Awful screams from the cellars could be heard even at the top of the tower. Princess Luna's rosy cheeks were now very pale and it seemed as if she would fade away long before the executioner laid her on the block. The heavy rain stopped late in the night and the silence of death already ruled in their room. One of the moon Goddess's faces shone outside the window opening and a silver beam came in. Shelana and Midar slept, but Jomar and Luna didn't.

"You see the beautiful moonlight"? he whispered.

"I called you Luna because you looked so beautiful when the moon shone on you".

Poor Luna didn't bother to listen. She had given up all hope, but Jomar gave her a shaking.

"Listen to me Luna. I haven't reared you and loved you in order that you should die when only a child. My own life and your mother's life will soon be over, but I want you and Midar to live. There is still a chance to save you both. If you hide under our corpses in our coffins the soldiers will carry you out to safety. You will leave your clothes behind and fill them with straw so that you appear to be asleep".

"It will not succeed", muttered Luna.

"Listen, I know the Murtsch-Takesjdell people's rituals. When they bury beheaded prisoners, they always let the coffins stay out in the open for one night before lowering them into the ground so that the souls can be collected by Satan. This means that you should be able to open the lids and flee into the forest. I know that you are a brave girl Luna. An angel gave you the gift of courage".

"I won't do it. I don't want to live without you and mother. Find a way to save us all"!

"You will do as I say. It is thanks to the fact that Inkyshade is so evil that you have got this chance. The sagas usually tell us that the tyrants are destroyed by their own cruelty and perhaps it is so in reality".

Luna didn't answer.

"If you don't obey me then you obey Inkyshade instead. Do you want to die at his command"?

"Yes, I do"!

"Silly child! You have no right to think about yourself. Our people need a brave Princess and an equally brave prince to lead them in their fight for freedom. I knew you would become somebody great Luna. I knew it when you were born".

The moonlight fell on Luna's curly hair. Jomar had tried his best *to convert her and was on the verge of tears.*

Suddenly, quite suddenly, Luna solemnly promised her father that she and Midar would take this very last chance to avoid being executed by the worst criminal on the planet: emperor Inkyshade.

FOUR BODIES AND TWO HEADS

Luna's father put something cold and round in her hand. When she held it the moonlight she jumped with horror. He had given her a transparent stone containing a horrid black spider and the light gave the stone a delicate red glow. Luna dropped it as she didn't like the spider, but Jomar picked it up and pressed it in her palm.

"You mustn't be afraid of this stone, he said harshly".

"The spider died a very long time ago and is embedded in amber. This stone will give you magic powers and you will be lost without it, so you must never lose it. Promise me that".

Luna promised to take good care of it even though the spider frightened her.

"When I was about your age I was very ill with a high fever. The doctor said he couldn't save me and my father cried for the first time in his life. However, and old quack came to the Palace and placed this amber in my hand. Anyway, within a day I was well. I had to promise her to take good care of the stone and not give it away until the night before my death and that night has now arrived. The amber is yours and I hope it will save your life in the same way as it has, until now, saved mine".

She held the stone once more in the moonlight and looked at the repulsive spider.

"Are you certain that the amber will protect me? She asked anxiously".

"Perhaps its power is evil and will destroy me"!

"Don't be afraid Luna. It is only bad to your enemies. You can rely on me completely".

She then crept under the straw and slept with the strange amber in her clenched hand. But Jomar lay awake and was worried. Even though he himself was not afraid of death; it was the children he was concerned about. It grieved him that he would never know whether they had managed to flee. When it was time for them to try to escape he would be a lifeless corpse.

Even if Jomar believed in the amber's protective power, he had reason to be worried. He had not told Luna the whole truth. Strange things had sometimes happened with the stone, which he didn't understand. The spider could disappear for a few seconds and be replaced by the old quack's face. A chuckling laugh was then heard from the amber and shortly afterwards something tragic always occurred, but it had only happened four times during his life. However, he was convinced it was right to give the stone to Luna. He felt that one of these days it would save her life.

The dawn came and the royal family was wakened by the tramp of steps as two executioners, dressed in black,, came up the narrow tower stairs to the room. Luna screamed in despair and Midar began to cry. The children understood that the executioners were on the way to fetch their parents. Jomas held Luna's hand for the last time. She clung to his arm and looked at him with burning tears in her eyes.

"Death will now take me away from you my dearest darling daughter", he said in his softest voice.

"In a few minutes it will be you who must take responsibility for your little brother. I want you to keep the amber not only for its power, but also as a memory of me".

"Every time you long for your dead father you shall squeeze the stone".

"I don't want to", sobbed Luna.

"Please, please stay with me dear mother and father"!

At the same instant the iron door was opened and the two executioners tramped in. They wore black hoods with eyeholes to avoid being recognized. However, Jomar thought he recognized their eyes and ripped their hoods off. The men tried to stop him but he was stronger. They were two of his own guardsmen.

"Traitors"! He shouted.

"You have sworn to be loyal and now you are going to execute me. Someday you will get a traitor's reward".

"Don't cause trouble now Jomar or it will be worse for you, said one of the executioners".

"Inkyshade may decide to use a more unpleasant method of execution".

Luna gave the executioner a kick on his leg which made him swear and he pushed her so violently that she fell, but fortunately the hay saved her from injury.

"Murderer"! Screamed the unhappy Luna.

"I shall have my revenge on you".

"Shall you indeed"? Said the executioner scornfully.

"Don't you know that you also are condemned to death? Perhaps you think that you can hit us on the head with your gravestone"?

Jomar nodded approvingly to his daughter as if to let her know that he wanted her to avenge his death. He then took Shelana's hand and went down the steps. He knew it was pointless to cause more trouble, but Shelana was not so calm. She spat on the executioners and cursed them.

"Why have you deserted your own country"? She screamed.

"Hold your tongue woman", shouted one of the executioners.

"You are dethroned and no longer have any voice in affairs. Cestrelle needs law and order and we can only get it with the emperor's help".

He pulled the black hood over his head and turned towards King Jomar:

"You have been a weak and miserable King; you don't deserve to have loyal soldiers".

The children screamed and cried when they heard the axe fall. Twice it fell on the block and it was all over. Jomar was compelled to watch Shelana's execution and then it was his turn to kneel and bend his head forward. He had promised himself to die with a smile, but he couldn't and before the cruel blow he called his beloved Luna's name.

Luuna! Luuna! Echoed in the fort.

Such vile cruelty on the part of the evil Inkyshade was a curse on the whole of mankind. Midar cried for several hours and Luna hugged him like a mother. She dried his tears, showed him the amber and told him not to be afraid of his parent's corpses. Midar was scared out of his senses but Luna was strong and brave and she talked him out of it.

"Only the coffin can save us Midar, she repeated over and over again".

"I love you and you must do exactly as I say, you must".

It was evening and their miserable supper was thrown in through the opening in the iron door. Midar wasn't hungry but Luna succeeded in persuading him to eat.

"You must eat", she said.

"You must be big and strong so that you can help to kill many of our enemies".

The cold evening air entered their room and the royal children froze. They needed warm porridge but the mean Inkyshade only allowed them salt meat and salt herring. Late in the evening the iron door was unlocked and a black coffin was carried in by the executioners. Their parents' heads had been nailed to its lid. The horrible executioners sneered at the poor children and wished them sweet dreams. Luna tried, but couldn't hold back her tears in the face of such barbarity. Her mother and father were headless inside the coffin.

Luna was unable to sleep during this horrible night. She knew there was a risk that their attempt to escape might fail. Although her father hadn't said so, she understood there was a possibility that they might be buried alive.

One of the moons shone outside the window opening. Luna held the amber in the moonlight and looked for a long time at the spider. Twice she was almost certain it moved.

"Are you inside the amber, father"? Is mother there also? She whispered very sadly.

The stone changed colour and frightened her so she put it back in her pocket.

She looked at the moon, which was almost full. Perhaps the moon Goddess wanted to say something to the little girl who bore one of her many names. Poor Luna knelt and clasped her hands in prayer.

"Oh Hindladrim, Goddess of the moons, you know I love the white light from your four faces. I respect you as much as I respect the Mother of creation. If you love me, help me to escape from the soldiers and this awful fort. Let my brother live and be happy".

Luna knew it was a serious blasphemy to respect the moon Goddess as much as the Mistress of the heavens, but it didn't worry her. She had always been free in her relationships to the mighty beings of the heavens. According to the holy sagas, no God or Goddess could be compared with the grand Tismina. She stood above all others as she alone had created everything including, unfortunately, evil. This caused Luna to be less enamoured of her.

The dawn came. The children took off their outer clothes and Luna filled them with straw. It looked just as if they lay and slept in the straw so now they could only hope that the soldiers wouldn't investigate further.

Midar had wanted to keep his light blue shirt with the embroidered royal gold crown, but Luna explained why this was impossible if they were to avoid capture later on.

Luna told Midar that he must be as quiet as a mouse; he mustn't cough or sneeze. If the soldiers heard the least sound they would be lost. Then they climbed into the coffin. It was very unpleasant. Shelana and Jomar were ice-cold and the smell of death was awful. They had to wait an intolerably long time, but eventually the tramp of feet could be heard again on the steps of the tower.

Luna and Midar were pitched here and there when the soldiers lifted the coffin onto their shoulders, but the children didn't make the least sound.

The soldiers cursed the weight of it. However, it didn't occur to them to investigate the matter. They only glanced at the straw filled clothes.

"The royal children are really lazy. Soon they will sleep forever and yet they sleep early in the morning", said one of them.

"It's their problem if they want to sleep away their last hours", said the other.

The soldiers cursed all the way down the steps.

Luna and Midar were afraid they would drop the coffin, but finally, it was placed safely on the ground and Luna squeezed hard on the amber.

She heard voices. Several soldiers stood nearby for a long time and the children were compelled to lie still and wait. When the voices finally stopped, Luna took her father's ice-cold hand and whispered tearfully:

"Farewell dear father. I shall never forget you, nor your dear mother"!

She lifted the lid of the coffin carefully and looked out. At first she was dazzled by the light, but soon she could see the dull grey wall of the yard.

Luna decided they must go at once. It was now or never. They rushed out and sneaked along the wall.

Some of the soldiers stood in a group and one of them saw the children enter the gateway but he pretended he hadn't.

The heavy grating was down. However, they could just manage to press themselves between two iron bars and they ran over the drawbridge to freedom. They were so exited that their legs would hardly carry them. Then they were discovered.

"Two children are escaping", called a soldier from the watchtower.

"Let them go", called another.

"We have imprisoned so many people it's good for us if some escape".

Nobody could believe that they were the royal children.

Luna and Midar stumbled laboriously through the beautiful beech forest and their heels had already begun to bleed. But they were free. They were free to escape in their enslaved but dearly beloved land.

The archers and the moon Goddess

Luna and Midar had to make their way over many obstacles. They stumbled several times, but they got up at once and went on. They wanted to get as far away from the fort as possible in order to reduce the risk of being caught. Finally, they had to take a short rest and they stopped under an old oak with thick moss on its trunk. Midar had a pain in his foot and Luna thought he had sprained his ankle, but he was all right; just a little blood form a cut.

They went on and came across a lonely cottage in the forest. Luna broke a window and climbed in. There was no food, but she found clothes in an old chest and they each put on a thick sheepskin jersey.

"It is fortunate that I am the Crown Princess and can take whatever I want", she thought.

"Every article of clothing belongs to me. Even the window belongs to me, so I haven't done anything wrong"!

During this time their escape from the tower was discovered and the emperor had been informed.

"The children must be captured and executed", he bawled.

"If you don't return with their heads before the evening I shall order you all to be killed".

The hunt had begun. Two hundred soldiers, together with many dogs, went out on the search.

Luna and Midar climbed a hill in order to survey their surroundings from the top. In the west they could see the moors, a town and the sea. It was nearly all forest in the east and Luna decided they should go that way. Perhaps they could make contact with the King's soldiers; those who still resisted the greatly superior forces of the emperor.

By sunset they were still free, but the distant barking of dogs and voices made them run further into the unknown along mysterious tracks which perhaps had only been used by trolls. Only one of the four moons shone in the darkening sky.

"I hope we can take a brief rest now", begged Midar.

"Another moon will then have time to come up. It is so dark in the forest".

Luna didn't answer him, but the barking dogs did.

Later, when the barking had stopped, the moon Goddess smiled at the royal children with two crescents in addition to the face of a full moon. It was a night of three moons and perhaps the fourth would also have time to come up.

The children climbed yet another hill and then sat on a flat rock clearly visible in the moonlight.

Three imperial archers saw them and shot their arrows, but they were too far away. Luna screamed. She had thought the danger was over. Midar felt unable to go any further and Luna wouldn't leave him. They sat still and awaited their fate, hand in hand.

Their pursuers ran down an oak covered slope and came closer to the hill. They soon reached a large flat rock only a stone's throw from the top and tried to aim at the children, but it had become darker when they moved their position and now it was too late. The men looked up at the sky in anger.

The moon Goddess had gone. The crescents were hidden by cloud and the full moon was a pale dusky red.

"Damned moon"! they howled furiously.

Why should it be a lunar eclipse just now?

They shot their arrows without seeing properly and one hit the flat rock very close to Luna and Midar.

A terrific flash of lightening came down immediately on the three men and killed them all.

Princess Luna then knew that her love of the moon Goddess, Hindladrim, was returned.

In the surrounding countryside hundreds of estates, farms and cottages were being searched by the enemy soldiers. The pursuit of the children had been intensified. Luna and Midar had so far managed well, but Luna understood that their future chances of survival was, nevertheless, exceedingly small. The emperor had made himself into an omnipotent god. All those that he wanted to kill would, in all probability, be dealt with in a very short time.

"You must fight like an animal Luna", said a ghostlike inner voice which seemed to come from the grave.

"I know you always do your best, but now even that won't be enough. You must do more than your best, otherwise you will die, my sweet little girl".

Luna shuddered and got up. She carried her exhausted brother down the hill and into the forest. Midar was so ashamed that he found new energy and began to go unaided.

The barking of the dogs echoed again in the night. The repulsive animals would sniff and sniff until they found the children and then rip their guts out. Some idiot had said that the dog is man's best friend.

"The dog is the emperor's best friend", thought Luna bitterly.

The children found something like a path and continued to go further away from the fort through the increasing darkness, but the barking came slowly but surely closer to them.

It began to rain, first a few drops and then it poured heavily. The trees thinned out and bare rocks lay in front. They had reached a long lake and must swim across deep water, which looked anything but inviting.

"At least it will be a problem for the dogs", thought Luna.

"And it is better to drown than have the face eaten by dogs".

The heavy shower stopped when the children waded out. They swam with their jerseys on as they didn't want to give their pursuers an unnecessary clue. At the same time, the emperor's men were riding round the country telling the people that two fair-haired children, a girl and her younger brother, were being searched for.

Richard Terrain
ETERNAL DARKNESS

They rode as far as the front line, which was still held by some of King Jomar's soldiers. Of course they didn't say that the children were going to be executed immediately! On the contrary, people were told that they were going to be returned to their anxious mother.

After an unpleasant swim over pitch-black water, Luna and Midar came ashore on an unknown beach. The barking of dogs and the voices of soldiers tormented their consciousness. But now they must take a short rest.

Luna had swum with the amber in her mouth to prevent losing it. The sky had cleared up; the stars appeared and the moon shone on the wild strawberry leaves and white wild strawberry flowers. That white wild strawberry flower, the symbol of their native land, which meant love and called for patriotic courage. But the army was being crushed and there was hardly any native soil left to defend. The white petals were all that remained of independence, Inkyshade's soldiers had seized nearly all the land. He could compel people to lower the Cestrellen flag, but he couldn't prevent the white wild strawberry flowers from gleaming on the slopes every year. Princess Luna was convinced that nature stood on the side of the good people.

Two black ravens flew through the night sky towards the largest moon. It could have been an omen. It could even have been something as fantastic as a promise of help from a mighty God on another planet, far away in outer space. But it wasn't anything that Luna knew about. She only had a mysterious hunch that there was an unknown God somewhere in the infinite distance, that fought against tyranny and wanted the best for her and all other children.

Luna and Midar pressed as much water as they could out of their jerseys and continued their flight through the forest; shivering and suffering in the cold night air.

Thirty minutes later, imperial soldiers stood on the beach where the children had rested. Luna and Midar understood that they must soon find a warm house and kind people who would feed them and give them dry clothes and protection, otherwise things would go badly.

The soldiers of the cruel emperor also knew this.

DEATH BROODS IN THE FOREST

Luna and Midar were too tired to run any more. They walked hand in hand through a coniferous forest and left the coastal country behind them. Luna thought they were on the way to the interior of Cestrelle where the trees were tall in the vast forests. Perhaps there was still a free area somewhere in the large kingdom, which the imperial soldiers couldn't reach. Perhaps it was impossible, even for a large army, to control isolated villages deep in the heart of the forests. Luna hoped so, as she didn't want to leave her country. Her father had taught her to love her native land more than anything else and she wouldn't desert the land of her ancestors if it was at all possible to stay.

The night seemed longer than it ought to have done at this time of the summer. Two moons showed the children the way across treacherous heather covered ground which could give way at any time. All at once they sat on the moss with one leg dangling in the underground, but they were sensible and jumped up immediately. They hurried on before the small people could do them any harm. The moss was soft everywhere, but if they felt that they sank in it they chose another way to avoid any risks. Luna had a pain in her foot, but she was brave and tried to think about something else. When they came to a small marsh they rested for a while. Midar complained that he was tired and hungry but Luna said that they must continue at all costs.

At the same time as they sat on a fallen tree trunk by the marsh, a man lost his life in the forest some distance away from them. It was not far to the wide gravel road which connected the country districts and just then three soldiers galloped through the night on their way to the farming villages to look for the royal children. The third soldier was young and couldn't ride as fast as the others so he got left behind. The other two didn't care about him. He thought he was alone, but he was not. When he heard something move in the forest he stopped his horse and listened. He thought that perhaps it was a deer, but it might have been the royal children. Suddenly, he saw a man among the trees.

"Hallo there"! Shouted the soldier.

"You are not wearing uniform and have no right to be in the forest".

Those were his last words. An arrow hit his shoulder. He screamed and fell off his horse. In a flash the men ran up to him and stabbed him through the neck.

The invasion by the emperor with all its cruelty and murder had aroused an intense hatred among people in Cestrelle, but as they were overwhelmed by an immense military force the situation seemed hopeless. However, after their little sister had been killed, two potters from the capital city had gone into the forest intent on avenging her. They were the first to realize that this could only be done by means of an ambush.

They were alone on this occasion but soon the time would come when those who were Rebels need not be.

The children were still by the marsh and Midar was so tired that he wanted to stay and sleep, but Luna insisted that they must go on. She took her brother's hand and dragged him forward. They plucked as many blueberries as they could to help stave off their hunger. The cloud suddenly hid the moons and Luna had to guess her direction. She thought Midar was following, but when she turned round he wasn't there and when she called his name he didn't answer. She retracted her steps, but couldn't find him. It was all to much for her. She felt that her spirit, which had carried them so far, was broken at last. She lay down and cried.

Midar had been overcome by tiredness. Suddenly he heard laughter and harp music, which appeared to come from a small light glade in the forest. Perhaps Luna was there waiting for him, but he was too weak to go and see and his voice was too weak to call her name.

He heard girls' voices calling for him to go and dance with them and offering him porridge. He felt so attracted that he got up, but then he realized that the voices came from elves that danced in the glade. He turned away from them, but was met by gleaming eyes, which scared him and caused him to move again towards the glade. The eyes probably belonged to some animals which one of the elves had aroused in order to scare him, but when he heard a noise behind him he joined in the dance even through he knew he could be lost for ever.

The elves eventually got him into an underground cave and a stone door blocked the only way out. A mysterious luminous tentacle forced its way in and searched for him, but he avoided it. The stone door opened a little above him and he could see the stars. It was then he heard Luna crying and he called her in despair.

"Luna! Luna! Come and help me"!

A BLOOD STAINED HARVEST

When Luna heard her brother's call for help she sat up and wiped away her tears.

"Where are you Midar? Come to me, she called anxiously".

"I can't; you must help me! Follow my voice and look for a large hole in the ground".

Luna ran as far as she could through the trees. The sky was clear and the moonlight helped her.

"What has happened Midar? You haven't been bewitched I hope"?

"No, there is nothing wrong with me, but you must help me to get out of this hole", he answered.

Luna soon found it and with the help of the moonlight she saw Midar's face under her. He looked scared, but the hole was big enough for him to get out.

"Take hold of the tree roots", she said impatiently.

"You must hurry before the people of the underworld get you".

"There aren't any small people or trolls here, but it could be something much worse. It could be the opening to hell", said Midar sobbing.

He tried to climb up to his sister, but he was too weak. Luna was determined to save him. She bent down as far as she could and gripped his arm.

"Push up on the tree roots", she said.

With a great combined effort, they finally managed it. Midar ran from the ghastly hole and lay down panting under an oak. Luna followed and pressed his cold hand against her warm tear drenched cheek.

It felt better to cry by her brother's side.

They went in the glade, but the elves had gone.

"I thought you were dead", said Luna.

"But you are with me again and I have never loved you as much as I do now".

"How strong you are Luna. I didn't think you would be able to pull me up"!

Luna felt new hope rise within her.

"We must go on", she said.

"But promise never to leave me Midar. Perhaps next time I won't be able to save you".

"It was you who left me", he said and started to argue.

However, they had to rest and regain some strength before they continued.

Midar told his sister about everything he had gone through and Luna was worried. If she was worried, he knew that she had a good reason to be. They both shuddered at the possibility that they had found the opening to hell. They fell on their knees and prayed to the Mistress of the heavens for protection. Luna then saw that the grass near them was trampled down in rings, which meant that they had prayed in quite the wrong place, as far as the elves were concerned.

"What will happen to us now"? Asked Midar.

"Misfortune will come to us", she replied.

She hugged him and comforted him. Then they went on, hand in hand, through the primeval forest.

Suddenly, they came across a beaten track and not far away they could see the outline of a small farm with a light in its windows. The farmer was surprised when the door was opened and the two children came in.

"Where have you come from"? Asked the farmer in a friendly way.

"Please help us"! Begged Luna.

She looked imploringly at the farmer and his family. The farmer's first thought was that they had run away from cruel stepparents who had threatened to trash them.

They would never believe that they were hunted by thousands of enemy soldiers, some of them with dogs. But the farmer's wife saw intuitively that there was some connection with the war.

"What has happened to you"? She asked with tears in her eyes.

"Has the enemy killed your parents"?

They couldn't answer, but Luna's lips trembled. She wanted to say something, but couldn't manage it. Midar was shy in front of the family and as soon as he had eaten some porridge he tried to get Luna to go out again, but she said that they must stay.

A family of seven lived on the farm. All of them were awake and occupied with various activities.

Elona, who was the young wife of the farmer's grown-up son, came over to the royal children and took care of them. Midar sat on her knee and she pressed Luna's hand against her cheek. They felt secure with her and let their feelings take over. They cried for a long time as a result of all their horrible experiences and Elona comforted them as though they were her own children. She hugged them until they smiled and were happy again.

Elona was an intelligent girl and very fond of children. She had blond hair and a sweet face with a small mouth and many freckles. Perhaps there was also something quite special about her. One could almost believe that she was a farmer fairy who had achieved the impossible by becoming a human being. She was so beautiful that people in the village called her the Forest Princess.

The farmer's wife took some clothes out of a blue chest. She gave her daughter's old dress to Luna. Midar was given grey trousers and a little shirt, which had belonged to their youngest son.

Luna and Midar sat on the soft wolf skin in front of the hearth and warmed their hands. The farmer had killed the wolf himself. The family couldn't resist asking the children what had happened. Luna told them that the emperor's soldiers were intent on killing them, but she didn't say who she was.

It was quiet in the farmhouse. The family had tried to think about other things than war during the previous day as they had so much to do, but now they were reminded of the danger that threatened them. The farmer was the first to break the silence. He hit the table with his fist and rumbled in his rough voice:

"Damned soldier thugs! Have they no sense of shame? Don't they understand that it is a foul crime to kill children? If they come here I shall give them what they deserve"!

He gripped his axe and swore. Then he lay his large powerful hands on the children's shoulders and said:

"You are safe with me. I won't let any of that scum into my farmhouse".

"Now we know how these enemy soldiers are. They are not men if they are prepared to kill children", *said the farmer's son.*

"All soldiers are the same", *muttered the farmer.* "They never leave honest farming people alone. It would be a blessing if somebody killed every soldier in the world".

"But why are they out after you children"? *Asked Elona.*

Luna looked anxiously at Midar. Then she looked slowly round the family. She would have preferred to avoid telling the truth as she knew that death would come to them if the enemy got to know who they were. However, they all looked so kind. Anyway for safety's sake she stood up and asked with a serious voice:

"Can I trust you all? Are you loyal to the King and your country"?

The farmer felt hurt, but he understood that she had reason to be worried. There were rumours about young men who were willing to cooperate with the emperor's soldiers.

"Yes, it's clear that you can rely on us", *he said with an irritated* voice.

"Neither are we traitors like some of the rich people. Shame on those estate owners who have failed us. I was myself at the district court and raised my hand for the King. I won't desert my democracy when it is threatened".

He gave his hand to her so that she could feel confident in him.

Luna looked even more serious.

"Your King and my father is dead"! She said sadly.

"The soldiers have also executed my mother, but we managed to escape".

The farmer was startled. He looked her strait in her face and recognized her at once. She had the same blue eyes and light curly hair as the little Princess who waved to the crowd from the balcony of the Palace.

"You are Princess Luna and your brother is Prince Midar", he stuttered.

"And our King has been executed. Have these devils decided to murder the whole royal family? It must not happen as that means the end for Cestrelle. I shall protect you both. Nobody will hurt you. Now I understand just how bad the situation is".

Luna threw herself into Elona's arms and sobbed.

"Inkyshade has certainly put a reward on our heads and I believe that many thousands of soldiers are looking for us".

"Why does he want to kill you"? Asked the farmer.

"Does he think he can arouse anything other than hate and

hostility by doing that? If King Jomar really has been executed there must be an uprising. We are not going to accept the murder of our King. We shall pay back in the same way and I shall offer a reward to the one who kills Inkyshade".

He had hardly spoken before a soldier pounded on the door. Midar screamed but Elona put her hand over his mouth. The pounding continued.

"Let us in you country rats"! Shouted one of the soldiers.

"Open in the name of emperor Inkyshade"!

"Quick! Get behind the bed curtain", whispered Elona to the children.

Luna and Midar crept under the bed quilt so that they wouldn't be seen even if the soldiers pulled the curtains away, but their bodies trembled in fear.

The farmer stood at the door.

"Why should I open for you? You only want to steal and kill".

"Guard your tongue if you want to stay alive. I shall set your farm on fire if you make difficulties", shouted the soldier.

The farmer opened the door unwillingly after glancing at his axe, which hung on the wall. The oldest son took his scythe down and pretended to sharpen it. Two imperial soldiers tramped in with dirty leather boots and two horses waited outside.

"What does this mean? Can't honest people be left alone in their own home"? Said the farmer in anger.

"Shut up", shouted one of the soldiers.

"Otherwise I may decide to cut off your tongue and hang it up as an ornament to avoid hearing you babble".

The soldiers stood in the middle of the floor with their hands on their sword hilts. The youngest son was afraid and began to cry. The farmer's daughter sat him on her knee and looked anxiously at the soldiers.

"We are here to make sure that you don't do anything illegal. You know it is forbidden to own flags and sing the National anthem of Cestrelle. Inkyshade has decided that nobody shall be patriotic".

"Please we haven't had time to get rid of our flag", said the farmer's daughter.

She was very afraid when she looked at the soldier's long swords, but her father didn't allow himself to get scared.

"I am not going to get rid of my flags and I shall sing whatever I want", he roared.

Anger was getting the better of her father and he almost forgot that he had a family and the royal children to protect. He started to sing some of the National anthem in order to irritate the soldiers, but he was stopped by a hard punch which made his mouth bleed and one of the soldiers gripped his collar.

"Keep quiet! you yokel or we will take your daughter into the forest and play with her".

"No, father you must calm yourself down", she cried.

"Listen to this sensible girl", said one of the soldiers.

The farmer pulled himself out of the soldier's grip but he didn't hit back. He contented himself with a glance at his axe. His son sharpened his scythe now and then, even though it didn't need sharpening.

Elona hid her face in her hands, but one of the soldiers lifted her chin.

"You are a strange one. A fairy among all these stinking louts. I knew there was something wrong with you".

He looked at the large cauldron, which stood by the hearth.

"What kind of lousy food do you eat in this country"?

He shouldn't have said that. The farmer's wife couldn't stand anybody speaking badly about her porridge and she gave the soldier a resounding cuff.

"You should learn some manners. Don't you learn how to behave decently on your side of the ocean"?

The soldier raised his fist to hit the quarrelsome woman but his comrade stopped him.

"Leave her alone. We have more important things to do than quarrel about porridge".

The soldier stood and looked threateningly at the family.

"We have not only come her to check on you", he shouted.

"Our most important job is to search for two children who have run away from home and if we find them we must return them to their parents as soon as possible. Have any of you seen a boy and a girl in wet sheepskin? The boy has fair hair and brown eyes; the girl has fair hair and blue eyes".

The farmer laughed.

"So sweet and angelic", he said scornfully.

"Just imagine, Inkyshade's soldiers are so kind that they want to help in this situation. Of course you two soldiers aren't good enough for the battlefield. The most you manage is to search for runaway children"?

"Answer the question", the soldier shouted.

"Have any of you seen these children"?

"No, don't you think we have enough of our own children"? Said the farmer.

One after another the family shook their heads.

"If you are lying it will be worse for you. To lie to soldiers is the same as treason".

They began to search. The farmer was worried and tried to stop them but they pushed him brutally aside and he fell on the floor. However, he got up at once.

"What is the point of searching"? He asked.

"I have told you we aren't hiding any children here".

One of the soldiers gave him a suspicious look.

"What are you afraid of then? If the children aren't here it doesn't matter if we search".

The soldiers opened all the doors in the old cupboard, which the farmer's grandfather had made. 'Then they turned to the bed curtain. The farmer's son stopped sharpening his scythe. His father took down something, which hung on the wall and held it behind him. Father and son winked to each other and smiled grimly. The daughter understood what they intended to do and held her breath in terror. The bed curtain was drawn away and the bed quilt was pulled off.

"Here they are. We have found the royal children", the soldiers exclaimed together.

"Yes, you have and now you shall get the promised reward"!

Blood flew in all directions. Some splashed on the children. Luna wanted to scream, but couldn't. Midar thought he had been injured but found he hadn't. They saw how the soldiers fell on the floor. The farmer and his son yelled with rage and slashed into them again and again even after the soldiers were dead. They were like furious warriors who had eaten poisonous fungus in order to get high. The axe and the scythe were drenched in blood.

Eventually, they calmed themselves down. The children screamed and cried. The women tried desperately to remove the ghastly blood.

"You know how to handle an axe father. You did well", said his son.

"I said I wanted to kill every soldier in the world and this is a good beginning. Soon there won't be any soldiers left and then we shall have peace", said the farmer.

He took his son's hand in triumph.

"You were not so bad either with your scythe"!

"I can reap most things when required, but such horrible weeds I *have never reaped before", said his son.*

The farmer's daughter stopped crying and came to her senses.

"My God! What have you done"? She cried.

"If more enemy soldiers come here they will do the same to us".

"Don't be afraid, little girl. We shall wash away all the blood. Nobody will ever know anything, said her father".

He glanced at the spades, which hung on the wall and had a good mind to take one down and smash the soldiers' skulls for the last time, but he checked himself. He understood that the women couldn't stand any more violence.

"We should bury these two dead lice in the forest, don't you agree father"? Asked his son.

"That's what I think we shall do", said the farmer.

Then he clapped the soldiers' horses on their backsides so that they would run back to the fort.

It had begun to raid. Soon it was pouring heavily and washed away all traces of the blood left by the corpses, which they had dragged through the forest.

THE WEEDS THRIVE

Although the men had promised to remove all the blood from the floor, it was the women who had to go with their buckets to the stream and fetch water. The farmer and his son had a tough job digging the grave in the forest and covering the corpses with soil. The old grandmother couldn't believe that her son and grandson were capable of killing, but she was nevertheless proud of them. She remembered her own grandmother's account of the way the nobility treated the farmers and she thought the soldiers had treated the family in the same disgusting way. However, she couldn't believe that progress had gone back a hundred years in a few days.

When the farmer returned, he stood at the door of the farmhouse with her son and found to his disappointment that the whole family sat in silence.

"What is it with you all? Are you sulking when we have been so brave"?

He had expected them to be as happy as larks, but they were sad that the peace they had been used to was over. The farmer's beautiful daughter was the first to break the silence. She smiled at her father and threw herself into his arms.

"Thanks dear father. You saved me", she whispered in his ear.

"You must have understood that I would never let those soldiers rape my only daughter", he said and hugged her.

"I would willingly have died to enable you to live a happy life", my girl.

When her mother saw that her daughter was happy, she herself was soon in a good mood. She put some sticks on the fire and warmed up the porridge.

"Now we can celebrate that we have royal guests", said the farmer and filled their glasses with mead.

Luna and Midar sat curled up in bed with Elona who was already like a mother for them. The little Prince leaned his head on her arm and she caressed him to make him feel safe. Then she talked to Luna:

"It makes me so happy to hold a real Princess's hand. You are so sweet and fairylike with your blond hair".

- Do you know what the farmers in the village call me? She asked Luna.

- It must be something pleasant as you are so kind, said Luna.

- They call me the forest Princess. But you are a real Princess and I believe that later on you will be Cestrelle's queen. The emperor's soldiers will someday give up voluntarily when they realize that you can rule better than they can.

Luna sighed heavily. It worried her that everybody expected so much. She didn't think that she could manage to rule a whole country.

The farmer's son heard what his dear wife said and he turned towards her with a sad smile.

"I really hope that you are right Elona, but I believe that we must conquer the emperor's soldiers before we can be free".

"No", said Elona firmly. "I don't want any more blood to be spilt. If we are kind to the soldiers they will be kind to us. They will get tired of oppressing us and long to cultivate the land instead".
The farmer listened to their conversation but he didn't think Elona was right on this point.
"All that takes a very long time and I'm not prepared to wait so long", he said as he gripped his axe handle.
"Freedom is worth its price in blood. It's obvious that your family have never been serfs in the forest. It is difficult for you to understand what serfdom means, but I know something about it through my grandfather. He had a relative, some generations before him, who was a serf under a nobleman. He learnt that these estate-owners must be killed before they make life a living hell for the serfs".
"Do you think we shall really be serfs, father"? The farmer's daughter asked anxiously.
"I think Inkyshade is planning to hold us in serfdom", said the father with an angry voice.
"But I shall not let him have a free hand to do whatever he wants. It is an old tradition of the farmers to manage their own farms".
Luna and Midar were almost asleep in Elona's arms when the smell of hot porridge woke them up. They were very hungry and rushed to the table. The farmer's wife gave them both a wooden spoon and warned them to be careful with the piping hot porridge.

When everybody was sitting at the table she poured all the porridge into a large wooden bowl and soon the whole family was happily eating. Nobody thought about the soldiers and the killing. After the food she took out her most valuable possession, a porcelain jug with blue flowers on it. She had inherited it from a distant relative who was very rich. The jug was filled with fresh cream milk from the nearby large farm and everybody took a drink. The family used to get milk and pork from this farm in exchange for a number of services.

After this, Luna and Midar were so contented that they slept almost at once. It had been an uneventful day. The grandmother used to sit up all night. She hardly ever slept so she was able to arouse the family if the soldiers should come.

"What will happen to us if the enemy ever find the corpses we have buried"? Asked the farmer's daughter anxiously.

"They will be angry of course", whispered her mother.

"But they won't be able to tell that we have killed them. Nobody will ever know the truth. Sleep now my child". She glanced at her grandmother who sat quite still on a chair; then she closed her beautiful eyes and slept.

When morning co me the family had to milk the goats. Luna asked the farmer's wife if she and Midar could stay with them and she replied that they must. She had no intention of allowing them to leave, even if they wanted to. It was far too dangerous as long as the soldiers continued to search for them. Luna threw herself into

Elona's arms and cried with joy.

The days passed. Autumn was coming and there were red and yellow leaves on the threes. Luna and Midar remained indoors all the time. Under no circumstances were they allowed to go into the forest. They had to be satisfied with looking through the window and Luna wondered whether Cerrellian would ever be the same country again as the land she knew.

They were not unoccupied even though there were no books to read. Luna learnt how to crochet and sew and Midar tried to carve wooden ladles, but he was not very successful and often cut his fingers. They also became good friends with the farmer's youngest son. There were always soldiers in the village and a couple of times they came up to the farmhouse and looked through the window, but they must have thought that the children belonged to the farmer and went away. Luna and Midar were very frightened when they saw them.

While the children kept themselves hidden in the farmhouse, many changes had taken place in Cestrelle. The war had come to an end and the emperor controlled most of the country. It soon became obvious that the people would not be allowed to retain any freedom at all. Their new masters were opponents of educational progress. They despised democracy, but praised dictatorship. The cruel Inkyshade had all power in his own hands and he had decided to reintroduce serfdom. After one hundred years of freedom the poor farmers would be forced again to bear the yoke of bondage. However, this time it was for foreigners, which was much worse.

In the capital city of Lindby people found that their freedom was restricted more and more. First, the fishermen were forbidden to leave port as Inkyshade was afraid that they would try to flee abroad and he didn't want to lose any labour. Everybody longed for seafood and bitterness increased. The next step was to prohibit hunting in the forests. Then the Temple was closed. Cult meetings and religious meetings were forbidden. Ordinary people should learn to worship the emperor instead.

Finally, the gates in the city wall were locked. The citizens were now prisoners in their own city and were unable to visit relatives in the rural areas. Only those who tilled land outside the city were allowed to pass. An imperial governor moved into the palace. The emperor himself was afraid to live in the city; he thought everybody wanted to kill him and he was right! He took refuge in a fort north of the city and hid himself from the people.

But the citizens had a secret weapon, which was far more dangerous than all the arrows and swords in the world. They knew how to use printing presses and some of these were moved in great secrecy to a room in an old attic. Thousands of leaflets containing rebellious propaganda was spread around the city. These encouraged the population to risk their lives in the fight for freedom and many soldiers were killed in the narrow streets.

Unfortunately, the printing room was discovered. One of the youths, that worked there had betrayed his comrades. For this despicable act the traitor was rewards with bold and valuables by the imperial governor. The soldiers caught two boys who lay sleeping in the printing room, and with a red-hot iron they compelled them to reveal the names of all those who had distributed the leaflets. More than fifty young men and women were imprisoned. Half of them were put in the fort from which Luna and Midar had escaped and there they suffered a lingering death. The remainders were hung up in the Palace Park as a warning.

After this, the citizens of Lindby lived in mortal fear of being arrested. Those who were not afraid of death were seared of being flogged. It often happened that one of the rebels was flogged at the market place and his back was streaked with blood. But as long as there was enough food, most people were unwilling to risk such punishment and the resistance faded away.

The citizens were in despair at their loss o freedom. However, amid all their sorrow and distress something happened to cheer them up. A rumour spread that although the King was dead, their beloved Princess Luna was alive. She had fortunately escaped from the fort where she was destined to die and was now in hiding with her brother, but nobody knows where. Inkyshade was furious that he had failed to exterminate the royal family.

The people had loved Luna from the time of her birth. Every autumn on her birthday, thousands gathering with burning torches in the Palace park to congratulate her.

She was the Princess everybody longed for after a lengthy period when only boys were born at the Palace and now she was praised to the skies as never before.

She became a symbol for the people's yearning for freedom. The citizens of the capital prayed for her and made offerings to her. They were all worried that she would be taken prisoner and her name was on everybody's lips:

"Luna is alive and free! She has been sent to liberate us! She is our gleaming spirit and has restored our hopes! As long as Luna lives, freedom cannot die! Someday she will lead us in rebellion against the imperial soldiers"!

However, Inkyshade got to know about the people's dreams. He was furious and made the soldiers behead a blond girl with rosy cheeks at the market place.

As a consequence of this brutality, he thought he had smashed all hopes of freedom. Thousands cried openly in Lindby and people lost all joy in living. Many became so unhappy that they committed suicide. However, the old Nanny at the Palace let it be known that it was some other girl who had been beheaded and this was the beginning of the cult of Luna, the immortal Goddess from the heavens.

THE BRAVE FARMER AND THE SAD CHILDREN

One afternoon in the late autumn, Luna sat in the farmhouse carding wool together with Elona and the farmer's daughter. Midar was also there, it felt good to be indoors near the warm hearth as the cold autumn had arrived and the harvest had fortunately been gathered in.

When they woke up in the mornings the ground was white with frost. It was freezing cold and the farmer's wife had to hurry and light the fire in the hearth. The three girls had a lot of fun while they were carding, but Midar just sat on the edge of the bed and did nothing. The farmer's youngest son had gone to visit some other children in the village. Midar couldn't accompany him as there was a risk that he might be recognized by a soldier from the fort, so he had nobody to play with.

The girls tried to hide their anxiety by thinking about pleasanter things and laughing. The farmer had been called up to the so-called imperial governor who was then in the neighbouring village and that could only mean some unpleasantness. The imperialists had brought nothing but sorrow and suffering to Cestrelle. All they could do now was to hope that the farmer would return unhurt and that news would not be too gloomy. The farmer's daughter was probably the one who worried most. She was afraid that the enemy had discovered who lay behind the killing of the two soldiers. The rain pattered on the window. The frost had gone long ago, but it still felt cold in the farmhouse so the girls moved their stools nearer the fire. Luna was just as good at carding wool as the others even though she was only a beginner. Midar was disappointed that he had nothing to do.

"I would also like to card", he said.

"Why am I not allowed to help you"?

"Because you wouldn't be of any help", said the farmers daughter.

"This is a woman's job which boys can't learn".

"Of course I can learn to card. I think you are silly", he said.

"Don't be annoyed Midar. Father will no doubt let you help with something else when he returns, said Elona. But Midar sat in a corner and sulked. Not even Luna's hugs cheered him up and this irritated her.

The depressing weather also affected everybody. The farmer's daughter was increasingly worried about her father. Both the old grandmother and the farmer's wife had returned and in the evening Elona's husband came back with his young brother. The daughter couldn't hide her anxiety any longer.

"Father is in danger", she cried.

"We must go and help him".

She rushed to the door but her mother gripped her arm.

"You stay her! It is pointless to go out and search. You would only get lost in the dark".

"But he might not find his way home! Cried her daughter".

"You must let me go to the neighbouring village at once".

"Keep calm now. Father knows very well how to get home".

Her mother was angry that she didn't know better and told her off. Suddenly, the farmer's voice was heard. He swore and cursed, but his daughter was nevertheless overjoyed when she heard him and threw herself into his arms. However, he was so angry that he pushed her away. His clothes were soaking wet after his long walk through the rain and he felt cold, but the worst was the very unpleasant news.

"It is damnable to have to freeze my backside off for the sake of that blasted governor", he shouted.

"The imperial soldiers can go to hell"!

He slammed the door of the farmhouse as hard as he could; then he turned to the royal children and apologized for his language. He felt it was unacceptable to swear when Luna and Midar were at home.

"What has happened", asked the grandmother.

"You look as though you have met the devil himself".

"Those mean blackguards have taken our land from us", said the farmer angrily.

"When I arrived at the barracks I was told that the governor now owns my farm. I was so amazed that I was unable to say anything to them. And what do you think they gave me in payment? One miserable silver coin! My land is worth at least a hundred times as much and when I said I wouldn't sell they threatened co cut my throat. The soldiers stood around with their weapons and there were a lot of them. I met many farmers on the way home who had received the same treatment. They talked about rebellion and an armed fight. I told them that they could rely on my support".

"Are you completely out of your mind father", cried his daughter. "There are many thousands of enemy soldiers. How can a few farmers fight against them when all the King's soldiers couldn't do it"?

"And what do you think will happen to us if we don't rise up against them? How shall we survive without our land? That devil wants us to cultivate his land. We shall be compelled to compete with the pigs in the sty for the rotten remains of food. It is exactly what I thought. The governor is aiming to put us in serfdom and this is a problem, which can only be solved by force".

"For the Gods' sake stop and think", begged his wife.

"Dear Tismina please spare us from uprisings and bloodshed. There has been enough war and strife in the world".

"Can't we leave here and flee abroad", asked his daughter.

"Videnien is still a free country. We could settle there and cultivate the land".

"Never", cried the farmer.

"This is our home. Our family has lived here from times immemorial. We farmers will fight to the last drop of blood for our homes and our native land".

"No, you won't succeed", said his daughter sobbing.

"There are too many soldiers and you will all be massacred. You can at least try to make the governor see reason first. If you are polite to him, he may listen to you".

"Well spoken", said her father sarcastically.

"Tomorrow morning I shall go to the neighbouring village and give the damned governor a piece of my mind. He shall give me a paper declaring that my land belongs to me and if I don't get it he will go to the same way as the two soldiers who searched for Luna and Midar".

"They will kill you", protested his wife.

"Think about the children. You must be polite to the governor even if you don't respect him at all".

He calmed himself down at last when he realized that the women were talking sense.

They all ate the evening meal in silence. Everybody was worried and fearful that the future would be most unpleasant. When the fire had gone out, Luna and Midar crept under the warm eiderdown. Elona went out for a while and then came in and sat beside the children. She smiled at them as usual, but this evening her smile was sad and squeezed their hands as if she was afraid that they would leave her.

"This may be our last evening together", she said.

"What are you saying", exclaimed Luna and sat up in bed.

"I want to stay with you always".

"It probably won't be possible my dear. I believe fate has decided otherwise".

"You mustn't leave us", said Midar.

"You are my fairy".

He moaned and Elona stroke his hair.

"You mustn't be sad Midar. There will be many women in your life, whom you will love and you have your sweet sister as well.

"Why are you saying this", asked Luna tearfully.

"Aren't you fond of us anymore"?

"Don't be silly", said Elona.

"You know that I love you. There is nothing I want more than to keep you with me and if I only thought of myself I would let you stay. However, I must consider what is best for you and for our country. I love this country and I want everybody to live in freedom, but it won't be that way. The talk in the village today has been unpleasant. My husband told me about it when he returned from the threshing, but we haven't told father yet. He is already so furious that he can't stand anymore misery to get worked up about".

"Ever since the enemy came here we have only had trouble", said Luna.

"But now everything will be much worse", said Elona.

"We shall no longer be free. We shall be serfs and must move into the cowsheds with the cows every evening and be locked in".

"Is that true? It can't be possible", said Luna.

"Serfdom is something which belongs to history and farmers can't be enslaved nowadays. Cestrelle is my realm and someday I shall rule over it as the Queen. I want everybody to decide over their

own lives and have their own land".

"You are so sensible Luna", said Elona.

"Even though you are only a child you know how a country ought to be ruled. However, the imperial soldiers don't think like us. They have already seized several large farms in the village and locked the farmers in the stables. Tomorrow it may be our turn to move, but you must never be a serf Luna; the soldiers might recognize you. You must flee to freedom with your brother".

Luna flung herself over Elona and shook her.

"Come with us to freedom", she begged.

"It isn't possible", said Elona.

"I am married; I must stay with my husband and he must stay with his father who won't leave his home. Don't feel sorry for our sake. I feel in my heart that someday we shall be free".

Luna and Midar cried in Elona's arms. The sky had cleared and moonlight shone through the window, but it couldn't comfort the children.

"Do you know I was named after the moons"? Said Luna as she wiped away her tears.

"On the night I was born there was moonlight from all four moons".

Elona kissed her forehead and hugged her.

"No my dear child. Your name came from love. We speak another dialect in the forest and we say Luna to a person that we are very fond of".

Luna felt that it was a comfort in her grief to have love's name. Love had always been the most beautiful word she knew and as she fell asleep she whispered Luna to unhappy Elona.

The morning came but the children slept on. They didn't want to face the horrors of reality. It was pleasanter to stay in the sweet world of dreams. However, they woke up when they heard the farmer's wife clatter with the porridge caldron. They could stand the depressing weather and the cold of winter, but they cried when they thought about the cruel situation in their country and the farmers being made to live like animals. Most of all they were sad about the coming separation from Elona. They were tearful whenever they saw her. Luna was almost as sad as when her parents were executed but she felt that she could live on as long as she had her brother.

The farmer's son chopped wood in the farmyard; he used the same axe as his father had used to kill a soldier. To toil as a serf didn't scare his as he had always done so however free he had been, but he was really afraid to lose his wife. If the soldiers harmed Elona he would be compelled to defend her even if the position was hopeless. Otherwise, he had given up all thoughts of an uprising; it was pointless to fight with over fifty imperial soldiers in the village. However, his father thought differently. He was prepared to act as long as he had a knife and an axe under his belt. A night's sleep hadn't improved his temper.

"I am going to that governor in the neighbouring village", he said to his family.

"He shall know that we aren't willing to accept his criminal offer of serfdom".

"Don't", begged Elona. "It is already too late".

But the farmer didn't listen to her. He wasn't going to let a woman give him orders and he trudged off along the path. His daughter still slept, but if she had known what a dangerous thing he intended to do, she would have done all in her power to stop him. The family ate their breakfast without the father. His daughter was told that he had gone to the forest to cut some branches. Her mother didn't want t o scare her unnecessarily.

They had hardly finished eating when they heard him wailing and groaning outside. As it happened he had met the governor near the local village and immediately started to quarrel with his false master. He just couldn't control himself and he forgot that it was the governor who had all the power. The cruel person had learnt from his father how to treat insubordinate serfs.

Four soldiers jumped on the poor farmer. He had strong fists but they were too difficult for him and nobody came out from the village to help him. They knocked him down, tied his hands and feet and gave him more flogging with the notorious cat-o-nine tails than he could stand.

He called to his wife to come out as he didn't want the children to know how badly the soldiers had hurt him. However, his daughter rushed to see what had happened, but when she saw his deeply bloodstained shirt she fell on her knees and lifted her arms to the heavens in despair.

"Tismina", she cried.

"How could you make this happen"?

The old grandmother managed to stop her youngest grandson from going out by telling him that his father was not feeling well and mustn't be disturbed. However, Luna went out in the cold air and saw how badly injured the farmer was; he had lost most of the skin from his back. He screamed with pain when his wife took his skirt off and poured cold water over the enormous wounds. The poor woman cried for her husband but cursed him for not keeping calm previously.

His daughter couldn't face the sight of him and turned away. Her big brother held her with clenched fists. He was more angry than sad and hoped he would soon have a chance to take vengeance on the soldiers.

Luna stopped crying and stood beside the injured farmer looking very serious. He saw that she was sad for his sake.

"Have the soldiers done that", she asked.

He tried to say something but it was so painful that he cried with pain instead and his wife continued to scold him.

"I don't think that you have any sense at all in your head", she exclaimed.

"I hope you have learnt a lesson and from now on you will listen to the women here. You should at least understand that it is the soldiers, and not you, who decide matters in the village".

"I shall never be enslaved", cried the farmer.

"I am no serf; I am a free farmer".

"Keep you fantasies to yourself and don't tell the soldiers how free you are", cried his wife.

"You are surely not blind? You can see with your own eyes that freedom is finished".

He went down on his knees with a groan. He swore and moaned loudly because of the pain.

Princess Luna had stood motionless beside him for a long time. She looked at the grey sky and was deep in thought. Suddenly she woke up, put her hands on the farmer's shoulders and looked straight at him in a strange way. He looked at her and wondered what she meant.

"You shall live", she said.

"Your wounds will heal. You have been so kind to me and my little brother. I don't want you to have any pain and it will go away. The soldiers can't hurt you, as they are powerless. All men who wear uniform are weak and powerless. Only those who can make us happy have power in their hand"!

They looked at Luna with astonishment; they couldn't believe that a mere child could be so wise. And best of all, the farmer no longer felt any pain in his terribly wounded back. The farmer's daughter rushed towards Luna with tears in her eyes.

"You can't imagine how happy you have made me, Luna. You are not only a Princess. You are much more.

She hugged Luna and kissed her again and again. But Luna looked at her amber stone. It glowed with a bright red light and felt quite hot. Some magic power had flowed from it into her body. Luna was afraid that somebody would think she was a witch so she hurried to conceal it.

The rest of the family came out and wondered what had happened. When the farmer told them they stood round Luna and stroked her curly hair. They were convinced that she was an Angel from the heavens.

Midar couldn't understand why they were so pleased with her sister. Everybody was overjoyed even though the farmer had terribly wounds all over his back.

"How did you do it"? Asked the farmer's daughter.

"I only consoled him with my love", said Luna.

She had placed the amber stone in her pocket and it was now so hot that it burnt her skin and she was compelled to throw it out. Fortunately, nobody saw what she did, but they noticed that the autumn leaves smouldered at the corner of the farmhouse. As soon as Luna thought it had cooled off she returned it to her pocket.

The farmer's youngest son ran to the village. He wanted to tell his friends that he had met a real Angel. Nobody noticed that he had gone as they were so engaged in admiring Luna. However, he returned very quickly.

"The imperial soldiers are coming this way", he cried.

"They are armed and look fierce".

Elona screamed in terror; she realized that the lives of the children were in great danger.

The farmer's wife rushed indoors and found enough warm clothes, furs and shoes for them. She was nervous and asked her son:

"Have I got time to give them everything they need including food"?

"I saw them at the edge of the forest", he replied.

"It will take a while for the soldiers to get here".

"Be quick mother", cried her daughter.

She rushed into the pantry and put all the food she could into the two leather bags and gave them to the children.

- Hurry off now dear children. Run as fast as you can. Don't forget we all love you.

Luna and Midar dashed into the forest with tears in their eyes and disappeared among the trees. Their beloved family would never see them again. It was a sad day for everybody.

A LIFT WITH THE ENEMY

Luna and Midar suddenly heard voices. They had run in the wrong direction in the forest and were far too near the path. The imperial soldiers were coming straight towards them. Luna pulled her brother down onto the leaf covered ground. They hid behind a dense leafless thicket and hoped they wouldn't be discovered.
"We can't hide so near the path", hissed Midar.
"Be quiet", whispered Luna.
The soldiers marched past them only a short distance away and they sang in praise of the emperor. The children couldn't understand how they could like such a cruel monster as Inkyshade. When their coarse voices could no longer be heard Midar wanted to continue their flight. But Luna said it was best to wait a bit behind the thicket. It was too dangerous to run as long as there were soldiers' in the forest.
After a while coarser voices could be heard in the distance, but this time there was no singing. The tramp of high boots and the clank of chains came nearer and the children were shocked to see their dear friends coming, surrounded by soldiers. The eldest son was chained hand and foot. He had obviously irritated the soldiers. The farmer's daughter sobbed quietly and her mother tried to console her. Both Elona and the farmer's daughter were very beautiful and the soldiers didn't leave them alone. When an enemy soldier pawed Elona, she reacted by giving him a resounding cuff,

but he hit back even harder and shoved her so that she fell on prickly thicket and cut herself.

"You are a serf and shall obey", he shouted.

The farmer's son saw that his beloved wife had cut her hands and was crying. He rushed forward in anger and tried to hit the soldier, but he forgot that he was in chains and fell over.

"Don't touch my wife", he shouted.

"Leave her alone"!

The soldiers looked at him scornfully as he lay on the ground and stepped towards him.

"Isn't he satisfied with being chained", said one of the soldiers.

"Does he want us to flog him as well"?

"Chains are definitely not enough", said another.

Then they kicked his face with their leather boots and when he was bleeding round his mouth and nose, they lifted him up. The whole family was then compelled to proceed to their serfdom. The children had seen it all. The last they heard was Elona crying and sobbing. Luna herself was in tears and she realized that this was happening all over Cestrelle.

"I wonder how much our people will suffer before it all ends", she sighed.

"Perhaps this tyranny will last a hundred years"!

"It can't last so long", said Midar.

"There will soon be brave Rebels who will beat all the soldiers".

Luna hoped he was right. However, she didn't see how farmers *could be Rebels when they were all defenceless serfs.*

The autumn day was grey and dreary. A storm was on the way, but Luna and Midar didn't feel at all cold in the wind.

"It is fortunate that we have warm clothes", said Midar. Luna was not in the mood to talk; she only nodded.

They walked in silence through a birch grove between two arable fields and approached the outskirts of a village but nobody could be seen.

Not many birch trees retained their white bark, as the villagers probably needed as much as they could get. The black earth was already ploughed in the fields which would soon be covered by snow and ice. It was cold and it began to rain. Luna and Midar must find somewhere to live fairly soon.

The trees thinned out in front of them and they came to a wide gravel road. Midar was afraid of meeting any soldiers and wanted to go back into the forest, but Luna said that they could easily get lost there. If they followed the road they could at least be certain to get somewhere and perhaps they could ride with a farmer.

The road was steep and undulating and they could see the small village.

"I wish we had a warm cottage to go to", said Luna.

"Now I understand how life is for all tramps".

They continued on their journey and left the village behind them. Soon they came to a schoolhouse and noticed that the flagpole, which was an important symbol of patriotism, had been cut down and the classrooms were empty and appeared unused. It was obvious that the emperor didn't want children to attend school and be educated.

Luna didn't know where they were going, but they carried on. She hoped that they would eventually come to the border with Videnien and with luck there would be no imperial soldiers in that country. They went on and on; the road seemed to be endless and Midar was tired.

Suddenly they heard the sound of horse's hooves. Luna grasped Midar's hand and rushed into the forest. They hid behind the spiny branches of a big tree while a wagon loaded with wood went slowly past. Luna held her breath when she saw that the driver was wearing imperial uniform, but she instantly ran out and jumped on the back of the wagon and motioned to Midar to do the same. He had no choice and they hid among the piles of wood. They were worried that the driver would find them, but he hadn't noticed anything. Luna squeezed her amber stone and hoped it would protect them. It was still light when the wagon entered a village and stopped at a large farm. The driver politely asked the maid to give the horses some water and she went to the well and got them a bucketful. However, she only did this because she liked horses. If he had asked something for himself he certainly wouldn't have got it. She spat after him as he drove away. Anyway, Luna and Midar were impressed by his politeness.

The children thought about jumping off and asking the maid to *protect them, but Luna decided it was best to travel as far as possible on the wagon. They continued to move slowly through the village. No soldiers could be seen, but a couple of farmers who were chopping wood outside their farmyard, saw a girl with curly blond hair on the wagon.*

"It was her", whispered one of the farmers.

"I am convinced, it was her. The Gods have sent Princess Luna to our village and perhaps we shall soon be free". The other farmer was so shocked he couldn't speak the whole evening.

Dusk fell over the surroundings, but the driver continued his journey. Luna was surprised that he should transport ordinary wood such a long way as it was available everywhere. She was afraid that they would end up in a fort again and be prisoners. She told Midar several times that he must always be ready to jump off.

The evening sky was still fairly light when the driver pulled up his horses at a large manor. A soldier came and led them into the stable. Luna realized that they had been driven right into the lion's den.

The driver began to unload the blocks of firewood but he kept so close to the wagon that the children couldn't escape. The pile of wood, which hid the children got less and less and finally he couldn't avoid finding them. He was extremely surprised, as he hadn't expected this.

"How long have you been travelling with me you ragamuffins"?

An icy fear went through the children and they were afraid to speak.

The driver was quite old, but he had powerful muscles and looked unkind. He was angry and gripped Midar by his neck.

"Let me go", he begged.

"Don't be angry with us".

But the driver refused to release his grip. Luna was as sensible as ever and knew what to say.

"It is usual for children in this country to jump on wagons without asking", she said.

"Don't children in your country do it"?

Eventually, the driver released his grip on Midar's neck and glared instead at the blond girl.

"What are you saying girl", he shouted.

"It is all nonsense. Children shall not go out and travel alone. Now you can follow me to the governor. Don't think you can steal a ride with soldiers just like that".

He was just going to grip the children's arms and compel them to follow him when he stopped himself.

"I think I recognize you, but I can't remember where and when I have seen you".

Midar was terribly afraid.

"I don't believe you do recognize us", he whined nervously.

"You are probably thinking about some other children. We don't usually appear among people".

Luna gave her brother a hard pinch. She was amazed that he could be so stupid.

"Now I see who you are", exclaimed the driver.

He yelled with delight and turned towards Luna.

"You are no ordinary young girl", he said.

"You are that Kings daughter who has caused so much distress in the city. Those lunatics believe that you are some kind of God who will liberate them. First they say your name and then hit the nearest soldier as hard as possible. They can never learn that it is right to serve their superiors".

Luna remembered that her father had told her that she must be a brave girl. She squeezed her amber stone, stood up and stepped towards the driver. He saw the boldness in her face and was greatly surprised.

"You think you know best, but you do not", said Luna.

"It is wrong to surrender to tyrants and right to revolt against them. We shall never serve any tyrants here in Cestrelle".

The driver was amazed that a young girl dared to speak so defiantly. He was used to obedient children. Luna was so different from those in his country that he was afraid of her and took a step back. He forgot that he was much stronger and could have hit her if he wanted to.

"How can you speak like that", he asked with a gentle voice.

"You and your family were the authorities before we came and took over".

"No", said Luna.

"The farmers were always my brothers and sisters".

In a flash she took a block of wood and hit him on the head. He collapsed but recovered almost at once and saw the children ran away.

"Soldiers of the guard, come here", he bellowed.

"The Kings children are here and are trying to escape".

It was dark. Luna and Midar ran along the manor's white stone wall. Two soldiers saw them and followed. The children came to a corner and saw a small door at the back of the manor. Luna tested the door and found it was open. She entered; pulled Midar in and closed it silently. They entered a dark room and the soldiers' ran past.

"Where did the children go", cried one of the soldiers.

"They must have run into the forest", said the commandant, who had just arrived.

Luna and Midar sat on a cold stone floor and trembled in fear. Soon they heard the sound of many soldiers approaching and light from their burning torches came through cracks in the door. Luna could see her brother's panic-stricken face. She held his hand and whispered:

"Don't be afraid. The soldiers won't come in. They are too stupid to think about searching in here".

They heard a lot of noise from the soldiers and Luna realized that they were armed, but she didn't tell her brother.

The commandant then informed the soldiers about the situation and said that the emperor wanted the children to be killed, as they

were dangerous. A large reward would be paid for Luna's head.
Midar turned to Luna and asked her what they should do. Luna tried her best to keep calm. She wanted to be brave as always.
"We shall keep quiet and stay where we are".
Everything will come out all right, she whispered.
"We are not the only ones who have to live dangerously in the struggle against the enemy".
Midar felt consoled by his sister. She was so kind to him even though it was his fault that the driver discovered their identity.
"If I must die, I want it to be next to you", he whispered.
An awful silence took over again. Luna found some narrow steps and Midar opened a small door with a sticky handle. He looked nervously into a room and then shouted with joy. He had found the entrance to the pantry. Luna told him to be quiet as he could be heard. He felt ashamed, as he was always the one who led them into danger.
One of the moons had come up and moonlight came into the pantry through a large window. The hungry children saw the most delicious food they could think of: there were sausages, pies, cakes, cheeses, apples and bread. Midar wondered where it had all come from and Luna explained:
It is only Inkyshade's governors and others in high office, that get this kind of food. They have stolen it from the people who are probably starving. It is always like this in countries where there is no King to protect the people; the landowners also get power. Midar

didn't want to eat the food, which belonged to the people, but he was hungry and he changed his mind. Luna was just as hungry as her brother and they both ate so much that they didn't feel well afterwards. Then they found a small room with a bed below the narrow steps and they fell asleep at once.

A GOVERNOR MAKES A DISCOVERY

Late at night, one of the governor's maids came down the steps to make her way to bed. Her room was very small and was often visited by brown rats. It was extremely unpleasant for her to have such a room, but the sadistic governor would not allow her to move to a better one.

She had scrubbed floors all day and her body ached. None of the floors needed scrubbing, but the governor enjoyed seeing her toil, especially when he sat at his desk.

Before the occupation of Cestrelle she had worked for a rich farming family, who was always kind and treated her as a daughter. Every evening she sat with them for dinner and didn't have to serve at the table. At night she slept in the same wide bed as the farmers two daughters. The farmer had been a poor farmhand himself when he was young, so he knew that the work was hard, but his master had treated him well and he wanted to be just as kind to his maid. All the farmers in Cestrelle were agreed that the rich should not oppress the poor.

If it became known that somebody had behaved in the typical offensive manner of a nobleman, the village committee could order that person to be compelled from the village. When times were hard and there was shortage of food, the villagers shared. Everybody was regarded as a child of the heavens and the Mistress of the heavens loved all her children equally.

All this was changed with the arrival in Cestrelle of the immoral imperial soldiers. The wonderful spirit of freedom was killed, together with the King's soldiers.

Nobody was allowed to read those ancient myths, which thought people to respect the poor and weak. The emperor was proclaimed as the only one who could give people justice, but he was nothing more than a repulsive hypocrite and fraud.

The poor maid was not allowed to live with the rich farming family, who was so kind to her. The governor went round the village and selected the most beautiful girls to serve him at the manor. He completely ignored the wishes of the girls and intended to keep them for himself like cattle. The maid was tired and unhappy as she went down the narrow steps with a lighted candle in her hand and she opened the door to her small, dilapidated room with tears in her eyes. She didn't want to sleep in her bed as it was so small and uncomfortable and she longed for her farming family, but she was not allowed to meet them.

Suddenly she was shocked to discover that she was not alone. Two young children slept under the grey blanket on her bed and she knew at once who they were. The governor had informed everybody during the evening and he promised his maid a piece of gold jewellery if she could find them. She went out of her room up the steps and listened intently. She was afraid somebody might come, but it was quiet everywhere. Then she went back and sat on a dirty stool by the bed. She lifted the blanket carefully, without waking the children, as

she wanted to see their sweet faces and hear their breathing. She caressed Luna's forehead and hair and kissed Midar on his cheek.
"How fine you are, I wish you were my own children".
"How can anybody be so cruel as to want to kill you", she said on the verge on tears.
"Have these monsters no feelings at all? How will your future be my poor children? How can I save you when I couldn't even save myself from serfdom".
She stood up and looked in anger at the ceiling. Her tormentor was sleeping above them in his richly decorated room.
"You swine! You thought I would betray the royal children", she hissed.
"You thought I was willing to sell my soul to the devil for a miserable piece of gold jewellery. If I were a man I would kill you and your murderous gang".
The poor maid didn't know what she could do in order to save the children. She decided to let them sleep as nobody had ever disturbed her during the night. There were always many soldiers guarding the mansion and she hadn't been able to work out how they could escape next day. Perhaps she must keep them hidden in her room during the winter and let them eat her food.
She pulled the grey blanket over their heads so they wouldn't be seen if somebody looked in.
The governor was a rather young man with black hair and beard and a large ugly nose. He was the son of a cruel tyrant who had

taught him how to mistreat his subjects. He woke up in the middle
of the night and thought about the beautiful maid who slept in the
room near the pantry. He hadn't yet touched her, but now he decided
to find out if she was a virgin. He put on his uniform and went down
the narrow wooden steps with a lantern in his hand.

When he entered the maid's room, he found her asleep with the
grey blanket over her head. She seemed to be unusually short and
fat and he pulled the blanket off with a jerk.

"What the hell does this mean", he shouted.

"Who are you and what are you doing here"?

He pulled Luna's hair and made her cry. Then he gripped
Midar's shoulders and gave him a good shaking which made him cry.

"Well", he roared.

"Where do you come from and what have you done with my
maid"?

"I shall show you how I treat a tramp's children who roam
around on their own", he shouted.

Luna suddenly realized that he hadn't understood that they
were the royal children. She fell on her knees in front of him and
clasped her hands.

"Dear soldier, you can surely forgive us", she begged.

"We are orphans and have nowhere to live. We would have been
frozen to death if we hadn't found this small room".

"How dare you call me a soldier", he roared.

"Can't you see that I am the governor? Get out instantly and don't ever return"!

Luna took Midar's hand and rushed out of the mansion. Luck was with them and they weren't seen. They ran quickly through the forest trees but their wooden shoes were a problem so they removed them.

Back in the mansion the governor was furious when he discovered that the young rascals had taken food from the pantry. The children lay under a tree and caught their breath. The night was dark and through the branches they could see the twinkling stars. Luna was sad and began to cry. She longed for her parents, but most of all she longed for Elona who she knew had lost her freedom and was having a difficult time. She begged the moon Goddess to protect her and all other serfs against the cruelty of the soldiers.

"I feel cold", complained Midar.

"Which way shall we go now"?

"I have no idea", said Luna.

"We can't stay here anyway. If we don't move our bodies, we shall be as stiff as icicles by tomorrow morning. The cold is just as dangerous as the soldiers".

"My arms hurt", whined Midar.

"Do you think I am not in pain then", said Luna in anger.

"He pulled my hair and you know how sensitive my hair is".

Midar began to cry again but Luna was angry and wouldn't console him. She wanted him to feel sorry for her, but he only cared about himself. She wished that she was alone in her distress and pretended that Midar wasn't there. However, he cried all the time and wouldn't give her any peace.

"Why must I take you with me", she screamed in her meanest voice.

"You only make trouble for us. You could have stayed with the farmer's family and been a young serf". When he heard this he became so unhappy that he cried even more.

But then something happened which made him stop crying. In front of them he saw a small cottage.

"Look Luna", he called.

"Somebody is living there. We have come out of the forest".

Luna was going in another direction when she heard her brother. She would never have found the cottage without his help; she rushed towards him and hugged him.

"You make me so happy Midar. Forgive me for being so unkind. Of course I want you with me. Without you I would have died long ago of grief and loneliness".

"Me too", he said.

When they went nearer the cottage they could see in the moonlight that a small landing stage lay outside and a rowing boat was moored at the end of it in a lake. Owing to a mist it was impossible to see the size of the lake.

"The cottage is only a boathouse", he said.

"It doesn't matter", said Luna.

"You have made me happy anyway".

They went carefully out on the landing stage but they were afraid that some soldiers might still be in the vicinity. Luna thought she could see a faint light farther away on the beach; however, it was difficult to see in the mist. Midar was going to say something but Luna put her hand over his mouth.

"Be quiet", she whispered.

"I think the soldiers are quite close".

"Don't say that. You scare me"!

Luna remembered that nothing had happened when Midar called out and this convinced here that they were alone.

They returned to the boathouse and found that the door was unlocked. Both were terribly afraid when Luna pulled the door open. However, it was completely empty except for the twigs, which covered the earthen floor.

"If we weren't so afraid we could sleep here", said Midar.

"I am so tired".

"We mustn't sleep", said Luna.

"The soldiers may still be searching for us; we must get much farther away from the mansion before we can sleep".

They closed the door and lay down on the soft twigs. It was just as cold inside as outside and they longed for a fire, but there was neither a hearth nor firework.

Tiredness came slowly over them. They forgot their fears and only longed for sleep.

After a while Luna woke up.

"We have rested a long time now and should go on", she said.

"Just a bit longer", begged Midar.

A few seconds later they were both deeply asleep and their coats protected them from the cold.

They didn't know that soldiers, who would make sure that they would never wake up again, were approaching the boathouse.

THE CHILDREN DISAPPEAR IN THE MIST

Luna suddenly woke up. She heard somebody step on the landing stage and her body fell into the clutches of cold terror. She wanted to call for help but she knew that she must keep absolutely quiet. A soft light entered the boathouse through chinks and holes in the wall, but it was not moonlight.

"What is the point of searching in the middle of the night", said an angry voice.

"I don't believe that the royal children have ever been in this area. 'The driver probably made it up in order to give himself an appearance of importance".

"If he thinks he can make fools of us then he is wrong", said a hoarse voice.

"If it turns out that he was lying we shall give him what he deserves".

"But if we do find the Princess I hope he won't get part of the reward".

"He won't get anything. It is the one who kills the girl who is worth the gold. Inkyshade is not so stupid as to reward the wrong man".

"It would be fine to remove that Princess. The people seem unable to accept our authority as long as she lives. They think she will give them freedom".

"These Cestrelle's are really peculiar. During all my years at sea I *have never met such crazy people. How can they believe that a ridiculous young Princess has the power to hurt us? She has hardly learnt how to use a needle and thread".*

"The girl is dangerous", said the one with the hoarse voice.

"The masses adore her. Suppose a large army came her and put her on the throne. She would only need to point at people to have them killed. She could get it into her head to have us all killed just because we want to kill her".

"You are right. We must kill all those who threaten our power".

Luna heard everything. She searched desperately for a way out of the boathouse, but it had only one door and there stood the soldiers.

"Let us get away from here", said the one with the hoarse voice. "There isn't anybody here".

Luna's heart pounded violently. She sat still and listened but didn't hear any footsteps.

"You go first. I will follow later".

Luna heard one of them leave; the other stayed on the landing stage. He was in no hurry to go away. She then decided to wake her brother.

"The soldiers are here", she whispered.

"You must wake up but you must be very quiet. Stand by my side and press yourself against the wall". Midar did as he was told. The soldier heard a squeaking sound from inside the boathouse; he thought it was rats and ignored it. For safety's sake he decided

later to take a look. There was a slight possibility that the children could be hiding there. Even armed rebels could be staying for the night. He was prepared for the worst and drew his sword. He opened the door and tramped in, but he found nobody.

BASH! Luna had hit him on the head with her wooden shoe; he lost consciousness and fell.

"You are fantastic", exclaimed Midar.

"Don't be so noisy. His comrade could be in the vicinity. Furthermore, he may wake up very soon".

Luna looked around for a good escape route. She didn't want to go into the forest but she saw a rowing boat and decided to take it.

"Jump in", she said.

"We must leave at once".

She released the mooring and took a few fast strokes with the oars to get away from the shore.

Midar was so afraid that he lay in the bottom of the boat as they disappeared in the mist.

Luna had to do all the rowing, as Midar was too small. She felt pain in her arms but she was determined to continue at all costs, and she did. Midar sat up and leaned over the side. He looked into the dark water and wondered how deep it was.

"It is sufficiently deep to drown you if you fall in", said Luna.

"You mustn't lean out; it scares me".

"You wanted to get rid of me before", said Midar teasing her.

She thought he was being stupid so she splashed water on him with the oars.

"You will get more if you don't behave yourself". Midar sulked but soon thought about something else.

"What would have happened if the soldier with the sword hadn't been so short", he asked.

Luna trembled at the mere thought.

"To hit his back wouldn't have helped and we should have been killed. It must feel good to have a big sister"!

"You are the best", said Midar.

Midar was never angry with her for long.

He looked in all directions, but saw only mist and water; the only sound came from the oars.

"Which lake are you rowing over", he asked anxiously.

"I have no idea", said Luna.

"But I hope it is on the border of Videnien; in which case we shall soon be in safety".

"The lake seems to be very large. Can it be Angern", wondered Midar.

"Don't say that, Angern is as large as an ocean".

"It is a lake where people often get drowned in storms", he said.

"I once heard a saga about two children who rowed out on Angern and were eaten by a huge sea monster".

Luna was scared and splashed water on him.

"Stop it", he whined.

"Well, stop searing me", she said angrily.

Luna had become so extremely tired that she couldn't row any longer and had to lie down on the bottom of the boat. Midar was tempted to splash her but changed his mind.

A light breeze drove them on and a strange tiredness came over him. He couldn't keep his eyes open so he lay down beside his sister.

"Are you also tired", said Luna.

"Yes I am".

"It must be the mist", she said.

Something splashed close by.

"What was that", she asked.

"It was probably a fish", said Midar.

They both slept for many hours in a world of strange dreams. Luna was the first to wake up but she found it difficult to wake her brother.

The mist had gone and the sun shone over the treetops. Their boat had got stuck on some stones near a beach covered in birch trees. Luna screwed up her eyes in the strong morning light and saw several forests to the beach on the other side. If it was Angern they must be in a long, wide creek.

"Wake up Midar", she cried impatiently.

After a while he stretched his arms and yawned. He complained about a headache and pains in his back. It wasn't at all comfortable to sleep on the bottom of the boat. They talked about their dreams and found, to their surprise, that they were the same.

"Perhaps there was something in the mist", said Luna.

"Something with supernatural powers".

The sun climbed slowly higher in the clear blue sky and shone directly on them in their boat. It was so warm that they could take off their coats without freezing.

Midar still had pain in his arms as a result of the shaking he got from the governor. He had red marks on the upper parts and Luna blew on the tender skin. Hatred began to rise in her and she wanted to kill all adults who were unkind to children.

"I wonder how I will be when I'm grown up", muttered Luna.

"Will I be kind or will I be somebody who kills and murders people"?

"Of course you will be kind", said Midar.

"You are kind already".

She took off her long woollen stockings and waded ashore through the cold water; Midar followed.

With great effort they managed to pull their boat in and hide it behind the trees. If the soldiers should come, they mustn't find the boat, as they would then know that the children were probably nearby.

They were thirsty and drank rainwater from the crevices in a rock on the beach but they had nothing to eat. The leather bags, which the kind farmer's wife had so carefully filled with bread, had been left behind in their escape from the mansion. Their only consolation was that Luna still had her amber stone.

"I am dying of hunger", complained Midar.

"Now you know how the farmers had it in the past when the corn was finished in the spring", said Luna.

"It is just as well that you get used to being hungry. If Inkyshade becomes the ruler over Cestrelle there may not be much food at all in the future", she said.

They found their way into a beautiful birch forest. Birch bark could be used for so much but none of the trees had been touched, which meant that people seldom went into the forest and they would soon understand why.

The ground was covered with autumn leaves and in some places it was wet and slippery. Midar tried to balance on a fallen tree trunk, but it was so slippery that he fell off and wet the seat of his trousers.

They climbed up moss covered crags where the moss was just as green and fine as in the summer, but otherwise there wasn't much to remind them of that season. The birch trees had shed all their leaves and their branches sprawled against the background of the sky.

"I long for the spring", said Luna.

"I hope it won't be long before the trees are in bud". However, they both knew that the long cold winter came first.

They climbed slowly higher above the lake and under them they could see the stones where their boat had stranded. Fortunately, it couldn't be seen.

Midar was first to come to the top of the hill.

"Curse it", he cried.

"We are on an islet".

"Don't swear or you won't go to heaven when you die", laughed Luna.

The sun warmed her body and made her forget all her deep sorrows. She hugged her brother and said that she loved him.

-"I wonder where we are", said Midar.

"If the Gods are with us we have come to a free country without soldiers", said Luna.

"We can manage without soldiers, but not without food! If there are no people here, there won't be any food either", said Midar.

"You talk like a cannibal", she said.

They couldn't see any buildings along the shores. There were only forests.

Suddenly they heard a rustling sound from the thickets lower down the hill and they were scared. However, it was only some deer who had been disturbed when they noticed that they were not alone on their islet.

"Look", cried Midar.

"Now I know where we are".

He saw for the first time a black rocky hill, devoid of all vegetation, which was considerably higher than its surroundings coniferous forests in the east. They knew the map of Cestrelle from memory and were convinced that this was the so-called Black Rock; in reality a dangerous volcano. One hundred years before Luna was born it had been active. Red-hot ashes shot out and lava flowed down its sides and burnt hundreds to death.

"Well, we are still in Cestrelle unfortunately", sighed Luna.

"I had hoped that we were already in Videnien".

"How are the people in Videnien", asked Midar.

"Do you think they are kind"?

"Of course they are. Father used to say that the people of Videnien are our dear brothers. I suppose you know that Cestrelle and Videnien once had the same King. He was our great grandfather's father.

"Do you think that the people of Videnien will fight for our freedom"?

Luna shrugged her shoulders.

"They probably don't care that much about us", she said.

The children shaded their eyes with their hands and looked at the mighty rock in the distance. The forests south of the volcano seemed to be endless. Nowhere else in the whole of Cestrelle were they equally extensive.

It began to feel cold as they stood at the top of the islet.

"Where shall we go now", asked Midar.

"Dare we go near the Black Rock"?

"It isn't dangerous if the spirit in its crater is asleep", said Luna.

"But we can't go there without food. I'm afraid we must go back to the occupied villages. Starving to death in the wilds is at least as unpleasant as being killed by the soldiers".

"No", exclaimed Midar in despair.

"They would kill us at once".

"That isn't certain", she said.

"However, if we go south I think we will come to a large cultivated area where we haven't been before and the soldiers there will probably not recognize us. Furthermore, the boundary to Videnien lies in the south and that of course is where we want to go".

Then Midar suddenly noticed a rowing boat coming out from behind a tree covered point and imperial soldiers were sitting in it.

"Look", he whispered.

"They are on their way here. Hurry up Luna, we must hide at once".

THE WICKED AND THE GOOD

The children slid down a slippery rock and came to rest on the soft moss lower down. Midar wanted to go into the birch forest and hide among the trees, but Luna wanted to watch the soldiers and see where they were rowing. She found some dense dark green juniper bushes on the edge of a rock, which went vertically down the lake. They lay on their stomachs and crawled out as far as they dared. There were small gaps in the dense foliage between the bushes, which were just right for them to watch over the narrow channel between the islet and the shore and it was impossible for the soldiers to see their small faces behind the branches.

The children heard the stroke of the oars coming closer and soon they saw the small rowing boat drift into the channel. The enemy soldiers were very close. The two in the boat were only teenagers, but Inkyshade obviously thought they were old enough to go to war and they were equipped with swords and crossbows. Midar was panic-stricken when they stopped rowing and looked searchingly at the shore. He wanted to crawl into the thicket but Luna stopped him as she thought he would be heard if he mowed. They held their breath when the soldiers looked straight at the bushes and Luna regretted that she had allowed her curiosity to take the upper hand. The soldiers didn't see them, but they had a feeling that the children were nearby. However, they never suspected that their prey was hiding under the long juniper bushes.

ETERNAL DARKNESS

"It is hopeless to search for the children", said one of them.

"If we only knew which islet they are hiding on, but we don't".

"There are five large islets on this lake", said the other.

"It would take us many days to search everywhere and even then we might not find them. If they get into the large mainland forest, we have really lost".

Luna smiled to herself as she listened to their problems, but Midar was still very scared.

The soldiers continued to discuss their situation and their lack of enthusiasm for war service became apparent. Suddenly, one of them howled with pain. He stood up and then fell into the ice-cold water and drowned. A few seconds later the other soldier was badly wounded and collapsed in the boat.

The children saw a bearded man in grey clothes carrying a bow on the other side of the narrow channel.

Luna acted at once. She climbed on to a large stone and called to him:

"Who are you and why are you helping us"?

He was extremely surprised to see a young girl as he had always thought that the islet was uninhabited, but perhaps some lone hunter lived there with his daughter.

"I am a Rebel", he answered.

Go home now, but don't tell anybody that you have seen me!

The man disappeared immediately in the forest. Luna shouted to him to stop, but she was too late. He was too far away to hear her.

ETERNAL DARKNESS

Midar was happy now and dared to leave his hiding place. He was pleased with what the archer had done and wished that all those who had been responsible for killing his parents would meet the same fate.

However, Luna was angry and thought that the Rebel should have understood that she needed help.

"Our situation is just as bad as it was before", she sighed.

"Alone in the wilds without food and all because I was silly enough not to call for help".

She looked at the coniferous forest. Now she knew that people lived there; it was a place for people who refused to give up their freedom.

However, she wondered if it was possible to find the Rebels in such a huge forest.

"It must be", she said with a bold smile.

"We shan't go into exile Midar. We shall stay in our native land and be Rebels".

"Does that mean that we needn't return to those villages where there are soldiers", asked Midar hopefully.

"We shall not go to the farming areas", said Luna.

"Cestrelle must be liberated before we can go home".

"But suppose Cestrelle is never liberated; what shall we do then"?

"In that case we must stay in the forest for the rest of our lives. It is better to live there than die in Lindby".

They went hand in hand through the trees on the islet to look for their boat. At first they didn't succeed; it had vanished! Luna then realized that they were on the wrong side of the islet. When they finally find the boat they hurried to push it out and jumped in. Midar tried to row, but it was best to let big sister do it. They landed on the nearby shore and pushed the boat up. It was then they saw a frightful sight; a dead soldier was bobbing up and down in the reeds, face upwards. He seemed to be looking at the sky, but he would never see anything again.

They left the large lake behind them and took their first steps on their long wandering through the Rebels' forest.

"Are you sure there aren't any enemy soldiers in this forest", asked Midar anxiously?

"I promise you", said Luna.

"Would you dare to enter it if you were wearing imperial uniform"?

"No never, I would be shot instantly"!

"You see! The Rebels have power here and they are friends".

Luna and Midar soon came into a dense part of the forest. It was impossible to walk straight on; there was always something in the way. After a while they felt completely lost and didn't know what to do. However, Luna had an idea and suddenly knew the right way to go. It was as if the Mistress of the heavens had helped her.

At first the children were in a good mood, but they gradually became silent and serious. Hunger had begun to torment them; they *became giddy and wanted to lie down. However, they forced themselves to continue even though walking was a nightmare and every step was a struggle against tiredness.*

They found no berries to eat and the forest was larger than they had ever expected. They couldn't see a glade anywhere and the trees were dense. Midar was totally exhausted, but Luna wouldn't leave him.

Grey clouds, which had blown in from the sea, began to cover the sky. The air got colder and Luna shivered, but her forehead felt warm. The cold wet stockings on her feet and legs had made her feverish, but she was too weak to take them off. Midar was also beginning to feel ill. He had a bad headache and complained all the time.

"I was wrong", said Luna in tears.

"It isn't the Rebels who meet us in the forest; it is death"!

"I don't want to die", said Midar.

"I want to live with you".

"Midar, my beloved brother", she said in her weak voice.

"I shouldn't have coaxed you into the forest. This time I can't save you".

Luna heard a woman laugh. At first she thought it was a dream, but then she heard her coming closer. It was a young woman who was happy and giggled. She said something, but her words became whispers like the sighs of the wind. She couldn't have been far away, but Luna couldn't see her and her giggle came from different directions. Luna understood immediately who it was. Only the laughter of the treacherous Spirit of the forest could be heard like this. She wanted to harm people and used to see to it that the herds maids got lost and never found their way home. At the same time she was the children's only hope of reserve and if she let them lie there they would die of fever.

Luna tried to call for help, but her voice was so weak that she hardly heard it herself. She managed to stand up for a moment; then she sank down on the soft moss. She wasn't hungry anymore; she just longed to wrap herself in a warm blanket. She was wearing a sheepskin coat, but felt as if she was lying naked in the wind.

Midar lay quite still and his breathing was shallow. Luna thought he would never wake up again. She clasped her hands in despair and prayed to the Mistress of the heavens. When need was urgent only the great Tismina could help.

Time passed and nothing happened. The Spirit of the forest was silent and Luna became weaker. She sank into a partial slumber and thought that she could hear singing and bells. She believed that it was the angels who had come to fetch her and her brother.

Somebody gave her a push and she opened her eyes. At first she saw nothing but after a while she could see bushed and trees with bare branches. A lady of the forest with long ponytail hair stood between two oak trees. She was as beautiful as the dancing fairies. She didn't freeze in the cold air, as she was a supernatural being. She had golden bracelets on her arms and wrists an around her neck she had

a small bell which jingled when she moved. She held a wooden bowl
in her hands.

"Please help us"! Begged Luna.

"I am cold and feverish".

Luna saw how she smiled and giggled. She gave a bad
impression and Luna thought that she was wicked. Perhaps she had
only come there to see the children freeze to death. However, her
smile was friendly as she dipped her fingers in her little bowl and
knelt before them. She pressed against Midar, but he didn't wakeup
so she put her finger in his mouth. He tasted something sweet and
came slowly back to life. Luna was also given some and wanted more
at once.

"Eat dear children", she whispered.

"Eat my wild honey and get your strength back. Eat until you
have had enough and feel well".

They soon recovered completely and thanked her for saving their
lives.

"Are you really kind and not at all wicked", asked Luna.

"I don't like people walking in my forest, but I shall always
protect and watch over you. They say you are going to lead the
struggle against the cruel soldiers and I don't want anything to
happen to you".

Luna thought about all the children who had got lost in the
forest and met their death and she became angry with her.

"So you will take care of me, but let other children fade away in *the depth of the forest. Why do you care about the cruelty, which the soldiers are responsible for? You are just as cruel yourself"!*

She turned her back on the children and vanished. However, Luna thought she would get an answer to her question and she heard a distant voice, but it was difficult to understand except when the wind blew in her direction.

"The soldiers are the enemies of the forest and I want to destroy them", said the voice.

Luna looked at her brother in astonishment and he looked at her in the same way.

"I wonder what she meant by that", asked Luna.

"How can the soldiers be enemies of the forest? Of course they are cruel to people, but surely they can't hurt the forest and nature".

However, Luna had forgotten that people could use fire to destroy the forest.

THE BEARDED MEN

The sky cleared up and the sun shone. The children leant against an oak trunk and licked all the honey off their fingers; then they washed their hands in a brook. They must make contact with the Rebels before dusk. They knew the days were shorter now and the nights were cold. However, they had no idea which way to go, but the sun came to their help. It sank in the west and there lay the enemy, so they must go east by keeping their backs to the sun in order to have a chance of meeting the Rebels.

They were not at all tired and Luna wondered what the honey contained.

"It must have been bewitched", she said.

"Are we bewitched now", asked Midar.

"I don't think so. We would surely not feel so good if we were bewitched".

After a while they reached a small waterfall. A rapid stream hindered them from going east. It was too wide to jump over and too fast to swim in.

"Perhaps it is narrower further up", said Midar.

Luna decided to find out.

"Our only chance is to wade over it, she said. She took off her wet stockings and pushed them in her wooden shoes, which she threw to the other side. Then she stepped in and found that it wasn't deep but ice-cold and the stones were slippery. She went forward slowly and

finally dared to jump onto the bank. Her feet were so cold that she screamed.

"Come over now Midar and don't take long about it".

She shouldn't have said that as it caused Midar to slip and wet all his clothes.

"You clumsy clot! Now you have made a mess of everything. Don't you know it's dangerous to wear wet clothes in the cold air"?

Then she felt sorry for him and stopped; however, she never realized that it was all her fault that he fell.

The sun was still there, but not strong enough to warm up poor Midar. Luna offered to change clothes with him, but he refused, as he didn't want her to suffer because of his carelessness.

The pine forest was larger than the children had expected and it felt good to come out of it. However, they were afraid to get near populated areas, which were perhaps occupied by the imperial soldiers. They saw an old overgrown charcoal stack in the distance, which indicated that the wilds were not unlimited. The open areas made them think that somebody was looking at them whereas in the forest they felt alone and abandoned.

They walked into a birch grove where they saw a man sitting on a large stone with his back towards them. He had neither seen them nor heard them. Over his shoulder he had a bow and his arrow case lay beside him. His dress almost convinced Luna that he was indeed a Rebel. She shouted and rushed towards him.

"Help us! Whoever you are, please help us"!

When he heard somebody call he immediately put an arrow in his bow. Luna stopped at once as she thought he intended to shoot her, but as soon as he saw it was a girl, he put his bow down. He couldn't understand how a little girl could be so far away from a populated area.

His heavily bearded face and intense gaze scared her.

"Why do you scare me? Why did you aim your deadly arrow at me"?

At last he understood just how frightened she was. Luna couldn't know that in reality he was a kind person. He smiled behind his beard and stepped towards her, but he shouldn't have done that. Luna was so frightened that she rushed through the birch grove in panic. She wanted to get away as she was convinced that he intended to harm her.

"So silly of me", he taught.

"Now I have frightened her even more. Why is everybody so afraid of me"?

"Come back", he called.

"I didn't mean to frighten you. You can't run in the forest so late in the day. You will get lost in the darkness".

Luna stopped and looked at him shyly. He was clever enough to stand still and wait for her to return. He held out his hand and apologized. She hesitated a moment but then took his hand.

"You needn't be afraid. You can trust me and the others in the forest. We are Rebels struggling against the cruel emperor".

Richard Terrain
ETERNAL DARKNESS

At last Luna felt that she could really trust him. But she was annoyed that he hadn't calmed her before.

"You should shave off your beard", she said.

"Do you know how your face looks"?

He laughed loudly.

"Yes, I suppose I am always aware of it. But you mustn't be upset just because we are so bearded; we can't help it".

"You look like a savage", said Luna.

"I would sooner be a free savage than a tame serf. The imperial soldiers stole my land and wanted to treat us like cattle so I took my wife with me and went into the forest. When I heard you call, I was silly enough to imagine that you were from that soldier mob who had come to take me back and I put an arrow in my bow".

Luna now felt that she could rely on him completely. He was hunted by the cruel intruders in the same way as she was. He was a friend and he shared her misfortunes in these difficult times.

"I probably know what has happened", she said.

"Please, excuse me for being afraid of you".

"Don't be so sad", he said.

"We shall win the war and liberate the whole of our native land. Now you must tell me how you came to be with us".

Luna saw Midar hiding behind a bush and signalled to him to come out, but he was too shy.

"I come from Lindby and I'm on the run from the imperial soldiers", she said.

"I have my young brother with me, but he is a little chickenhearted as you can see".

Midar was angry when he heard what she said. He rushed out and knocked her down and didn't stop until he had pinched her. The man was happy to see them play.

"I would like you to stay here with us. You have no idea how dreary it is to be without laughter of children".

Luna suddenly looked serious.

"May we stay with you", she asked.

"We have nowhere to go".

"Yes of course you can", he said.

"We need a sweet little girl as a balance to all the untidy bearded men we have here. But please tell me why the imperial soldiers chased you. I didn't know that they wanted to arrest children! What are your names? Are your parents no longer alive"?

"We can talk about all that later", said Luna.

He discovered that Midar had wet clothes and Luna had wet stockings. He told them that they must hurry home with him to the cave and get warm by the fire.

"I intended to shoot some birds in the forest but I have had much better hunting"!

He led the children out of the birch grave into a dark fir tree forest where they met a group of at least a dozen Rebels. Luna stumbled over a root and hurt her foot but it wasn't serious. The Rebel with the bow lifted her onto a large stone so that all the men *could see her.*

"Look what I have found in the forest! She is as beautiful as a fairy, but she is a human being". They had never seen such a sweet little girl and were very pleased when they heard that she had come to stay.

"You are amazing Birmile. You intended to shout birds, but come home with a little girl instead", said the red-bearded Rebel chief Nilgar.

At last Midar came forward and the Rebels were just as pleased with him.

The children followed Birmile, Nilgar and the others to the cave, which was high above them on the steepest crags. They were so tired that they had to be carried up the last bit.

Finally, they came to a small dark hole in the rock, which was the entrance, and as they went in the daylight disappeared, but some distance in front of them a yellow light fell on the walls. They heard crackling flames and the giggles of young women.

"The men are coming", called one of them.

"Don't give Nilgar any food before he has kissed and hugged you, Ynisha"!

Nilgar caught up with the children and put his hands on their shoulders.

"Go in front and give the women a pleasant surprise, he whispered".

"But be careful! Don't stop off the plank because you will then

step into nothing. It wasn't our intention that the trap for soldiers would also be one for children".

Luna and Midar discovered to their horror that the cave passage ended in front of them and an apparently bottomless hole opened. A wide plank lay over it, but on the other side there was a rock which they could press themselves past. A large cavern lay beyond the rock.

The children thought that the hole was the opening to hell and it scared them, but Nilgar said that it wasn't at all deep. He had dug it himself and covered the bottom with a thick layer of twigs. However, it was impossible to see this in the darkness. It wasn't so dangerous to fall in, but help was needed to get out and no enemy soldier would survive the Rebel's help!

Luna and Midar made their way over the hole and past the large rock.

"I have a present for you women", called Nilgar.

"Close your eyes and don't open them until I say so".

The children understood that they were the present. The women were overcome by amazement and joy, when they saw the two children standing in front of the fire. They were far more welcome in their new home than they could ever have imagined.

LUNA, THE REBEL GIRL

The rebels lived in a large cavern, which they had turned into a pleasant home with a very high roof. Their fire was placed in a ring of stones and the smoke went out through a natural opening in the highest part of the roof. The children were happy that they could see the sky despite their position inside the rock. They soon discovered that they could also see another bit of the sky through a smaller opening at the end of a much shorter and narrower passage. This opening allowed fresh air to enter the large cavern, but only Luna and Midar could creep through it and for them it was a short cut to the outside.

The rebels had removed the sharp stones from the floor and elsewhere a long time ago. Woolly sheepskin had been spread around the fireplace, which were so warm and soft that they served as quilts even when it was cold. Barrels and chest had been placed along the walls and, at the far end, there was an underground brook with fresh spring water. On the other side of the brook the cave passage continued into the unknown.

The women wore sheepskin coats like the children. The Rebel Chief's young wife was named Ynisha. She was not only beautiful but also hot-tempered and more daring than all the others. She had dark hair, which she wore in two pigtails, and exquisitely beautiful brown eyes, which caused many men to lose their heads completely.

Ynisha was busy plucking a bird, which they would eat for the evening meal. Three other women sat by the fireplace and roasted birds on a spit. After the children had received their welcome hugs the women began to question them. Luna talked most but she didn't reveal who they were.

The women helped them to take off their wet clothes and Ynisha gave them dry sheepskin coats.

"Sit near the fire now and you will soon get warm", she said.

Twinkling stars could be seen through the narrow opening, but most of the sky was hidden by the rock of the roof.

The children each got a bird's breast to eat and at last they could satisfy their intense hunger which had plagued them so long. They had now found a home where they could feel safe and calm. The Rebels were so kind to them that they felt like crying and they were certain that they wanted to stay. Furthermore, the vast forest around them was still free.

When everybody was satisfied, Nilgar began to play on his flute. First he played jolly tones, but then the music became serious and formal. The forbidden National anthem of Cestrelle echoed through the cave passages and tears ran down the faces as they sang its beloved verses.

Some of them began to really cry and Luna was so moved that she couldn't control her violent sobbing. Ynisha sat her on her knee and tried to comfort her but without success.

Nobody in the cavern could avoid being reminded of the cruel efforts of the recent war, but they all hoped that happy days would return.

"They think they can enslave us, but they can't", hissed one of the Rebels.

"I would rather die than be a serf under that vile emperor".

"They want us to respect them as the authority over us", said his brother with a sneer.

"I would like to meet Inkyshade and tell him bluntly that king Jomar is our rightful authority and now When he is dead, there is no authority at all".

When Luna heard this she was even more upset and Midar also began to cry. The Rebels wondered why these words had such a strong effect on the children. However, Nilgar understood that it was the talk about the King's death, which was the cause.

"What is your name my child and who are you? You must tell me", he said.

"My name is Luna and I am crying because you have been talking about my executed father; my dear father who we loved so much".

Suddenly it was quiet in the cavern. Everybody sat still and looked at her. Then they began to whisper. They came up to her and felt her body to make sure that she was real and not a ghost. Nilgar began to cry for the first time since his early childhood. It took a little while before it dawned on the Rebels that Princess Luna was alive and with them. Ynisha fell on her knees before Luna and bowed her hands. She thanked the great Goddess Tismina with a prayer; but when she prayed she looked at Princess Luna instead of looking up to the sky.

"This godlike girl has come to our cavern. The Angels have sent her to us", she said.

Then she placed her hands gently on Lunas curly hair.

"You are alive", said Ynisha in her ecstasy.

"We thought you were dead, but you are alive"!

"We heard that Inkyshade had captured you and had ordered you to be beheaded at the market place in Lindby", said Nilgar crying. "But it was all a lie which they made up and used to force the people into submission. They can't kill you Luna; you are so great and powerful".

Finally, Nilgar managed to pull himself together and said with a solemn voice:

"From this moment Luna you are not only a Princess, you are also a Rebel girl. I have no palace to give you, but the vast forest shall be your home".

Luna was pleased to hear Nilgar say these words. At last her secret dream had been fulfilled and she was now a Rebel girl, who lived in the forest.

Ynisha took out a silver necklace with wolves' teeth on it and put it round Luna's neck. It was her most valuable possession, but she wanted to give it to her anyway. The sacred wolves' teeth possessed strong magical powers and she thanked Ynisha profoundly. She *promised to wear the necklace until the day Cestrelle was liberated. A long and difficult struggle lay in front of them and many lives would be lost before Cestrelle regained its freedom. They were sustained by their belief that tyranny could never last forever and that people's longing for freedom would win in the end.*

Printed in Great Britain
by Amazon